Cover Design and Interior Format

THE GHOSTS OF BLACK ISLE

OF

HIGHLAND HEALERS 4

KEIRA MONTCLAIR

CHAPTER ONE

Black Isle of Scotland, Autumn 1292

SHAW MATHESON STOOD atop the curtain wall of Eddirdale Castle, the sun dropping quickly on his right. He peered out over the landscape and caught sight of the person he was looking for, and a sudden shiver ran up his spine. Tara Cameron was returning from a quick trip to watch the dolphins feed at night on the firth with her sister, Riley, who'd just arrived for a visit with her sister and cousins.

Shite, but he prided himself in not allowing anything to bother him, but he failed in two ways. One he could accept—the odd feelings that coursed through him whenever he set eyes upon the lovely Tara, her luminous brown eyes dancing with glee from something she'd said to her sister. Even from afar, her vivacious personality shone like a star to him—her laughing mouth and the toss of her hair telling him more than words ever could. He was so drawn by the picture of her and her sister Riley returning from the firth that he hated to pull his gaze from them, but it was the lad riding toward him who caused a deep chill, probably one of the few people with the ability to distract him from his obsession with the beautiful lass on horseback.

Young Sammy represented the second issue he could not control his reaction to, no matter how he tried to force it away, coerce it to dissipate and never return. By the look in the lad's eyes, he knew something had gone wrong. He rushed down the staircase and out through the gates, swinging up onto a nearby grazing horse to ride out and meet him. Better to have this conversation where no one would overhear.

He could not risk revealing this web of lies at this point in his life.

He was nearly upon the lad when they both slowed their mounts and met off to the side of the path. "What is it, Sammy? There's news—I can read it in your face."

Sammy held out a scrap of parchment and said in a low tone, "'Tis another increase, my lord. My apologies for reading the missive."

"No apologies," Shaw said, grabbing the note and cursing under his breath as he looked at the number written there. "I taught you to read for just this reason." He'd been dealing with this issue for years, though at his age of one and twenty, he should be able to bring an end to it.

Why didn't he? Perhaps it was time to simply stop paying. He stared up at a hawk circling high overhead and considered his options but came up with nothing new. Pay or be exposed and betray a man who'd once been his best friend.

"My lord? Will there be a reply? I can wait." The lad of twelve winters was always willing to help him.

Shaw ruffled his brown curly hair and said, "Nay, lad. Go inside and get your meal. You've earned it this day. Eat hearty, and I'll join you in a bit."

His eyes lit up, and he smiled. "Many thanks, my lord."

"You should call me Shaw. I'm not your lord."

"Aye, my lord. Shaw."

"Hurry in now. I can hear your belly grumbling from here. I'll be behind you in a few moments." The lad rode his horse through the gates before he dismounted with a wave.

Hellfire. What was he to do now?

He moved into the stable and found a shadowed corner. He opened the missive again, making sure he had read it correctly. The bastard, whoever he was, was raising the price of his silence. How dare he? He'd just raised it four moons ago. Greed. There could be no other reason.

This was getting out of hand. He scratched his chin and paced the aisle between the horse stalls. He needed to come up with a way to end this— now and forever.

He needed to speak with someone who could advise him of the best plan, of a way to put a stop to this constant drain of his coin. So far he'd hidden it well, and the only one who knew of it was Sammy. He trusted the lad completely, but he was young. It would not be right to ask him for advice, nor did he have the wisdom Shaw needed.

Who the hell could he ask?

No one knew what had happened that day. No one except the man he suspected of being the blackmailer and Dougal MacKinnie. He and Dougal had been inseparable in their youth, especially in their teen years. But they'd made a poor decision, as lads often did, and now they were paying for that momentary lapse in judgment. Their deed had become known to someone, though, and that someone now used the incident against them, demanding coin from them both in return for keeping their secret.

He wondered if Dougal was being given the same increases. Perhaps it was time to talk with Dougal again, much as he hated to do so. The events of that long-ago day had ended so tragically that he'd done his best to eliminate even the memory of it completely. He'd stayed as far away from Dougal as possible, and their friendship had withered and died. But perhaps he would have some idea of how to stop the flow of money.

"Brother, d'you have a moment?" a voice called out to him.

He spun around and was surprised to see Ethan standing in the stable door with his hands on his hips. His stern expression was one Shaw saw more often on his eldest brother's face, not Ethan's. As if on cue, Shaw scratched his beard, something he did whenever he was uncertain about things. He kept his beard trimmed because he preferred it. The look from Ethan made him wonder where his eldest brother was, but Marcas was nowhere to be seen, probably with Brigid and his bairns at this time of evening.

"What is it, Ethan?" Ethan was the most loyal, most analytical person he knew. His reasoning was always sound, and he would never go against his clan or his family. Still, he had no wish for his brother to discover his secrets.

"I wish to know what troubles you." Ethan took a couple steps into the stable until he stood, relaxed and waiting, in front of Shaw. Ethan would not leave until he received his answer.

"Nothing. What makes you think something is bothering me?" He did his best to hide the guilt on his face, though it was unlikely Ethan would see it. Ethan was different, and instead, he had an uncanny way of *feeling* his guilt, a sense that most people didn't have. The chance of Ethan's not detecting the lie was as low as the two of them not noticing if a horse flew through the air and landed on their heads.

How he wished he had learned how to hide his thoughts from his brother.

Ethan's demeanor didn't change. "You're doing the same thing you've always done when you're worried, ever since you were a bairn. Your eyes get smaller and your fingers wiggle like you're ready to punch someone. *Who* is the question I always have. Who do you wish to punch?"

Ethan paid attention to everything. Sometimes Shaw thought he was too attentive for comfort. At any given moment, he could tell you exactly what the last person he saw was wearing, how long ago he left, and which direction he traveled in. Shaw, in contrast, would be lucky to remember what color hair the man had.

"Ethan, it doesn't concern you. If either of us could benefit from me sharing this with you, I would do it." There. He said it, and he hoped his brother would not be upset by his explanation. If he thought Ethan could help him, he would tell him the problem. While his brother was highly intelligent with an amazing memory of details, reasoning and emotions were not his best skills. One had to know how to think like Ethan did. He looked his brother in the eye, beseeching him to leave him be. His head hurt enough from all the thoughts racing through his brain.

"I think you're hiding something you should share with me. You know I can keep your secret. Perhaps I can help you solve your problem."

Ethan had that look that told Shaw he wasn't budging from his spot. Perhaps he'd underestimated his brother and Ethan was the one he'd just been wishing for, someone who could give him good advice. Sometimes he didn't give his brother enough credit for his rare intelligence. He was certain of one thing—Ethan would never betray his confidence unless the direct question was put before him.

Shaw took a deep breath and let it out slowly. "Fine, but let's go where there is no possibility of being overheard."

"Good. Since you entrust Samuel with your secrets, you should trust your own brother."

"How do you know…? Never mind. Aye, Sammy knows." He motioned for Ethan to follow him, and they walked out to the edge of the coastline, the one closest to them in Beauly Firth. They could see far down the shore both directions, and the forest was far back from the water at that spot, so he knew they were quite alone.

Ethan waited patiently once they stopped walking, giving Shaw the time he needed to consider his words. "Someone is blackmailing me."

"I'm certain you do not know who it is, or you'd kill them and end your problem." Ethan excelled at stating the obvious.

Shaw couldn't help but smirk at his brother's accurate assessment of the problem. "You are correct. If I find out who it is…" His fingers wiggled involuntarily, giving credence to his brother's observation about his movements giving away his mood, so he stilled them. How often did he do that?

Ethan never moved a muscle, not even a smile in recognition of his actions. His brother's unending patience only served to annoy him. He was so steadfast in his loyalty, and Shaw couldn't begin to be that patient with anyone or anything.

"Ethan, while I understand you'd like to know all, I cannot tell you everything. 'Tis a secret for a verra good reason. The blackmail has been going on for years, but whoever it is seems to need more coin of late and is insisting that I pay him more. I know not what to do about it."

"Stop making payments."

Shaw snorted. "That would solve everything,

would it not? But things are not always that easy."

"They could be if you just stopped paying. What they hold over you must be powerful, if you're so quick to discount the option. I know you, brother, and I can't believe that whatever they're holding over you could be so very bad. While I do recall clashes between you and Da in our youth over some lapse in judgment, you have outgrown such foolishness. And I don't recall any behavior of yours bad enough to inspire an evil mind to resort to blackmailing you."

"Mayhap whatever took place was unintentional." Shaw closed his eyes, thinking on that awful day so many years ago. His brother would be shocked to hear the truth. As would all his family. He couldn't allow the secret to get out, so he would do what he must.

"Mayhap you should consider the possibility that those who know you well would know the result, no matter how bad, was unintentional on your part." Ethan nodded for effect, something Marcas had taught him to do.

"I'm not sure of that, Ethan, but you've made me consider some options," he said, scratching his head as he paced a small circle in the sand. "I may need your help. If I can come up with a way to uncover who is blackmailing me, I'll gladly take any assistance you can give me. Until that time, I'll ask you to keep my secret."

"Agreed. I'd prefer to help you rid the land of the miscreant who is committing the crime, but until then, I am at your service." He slapped Shaw on the shoulder. "But, brother, the only other way to free yourself from his control is to confess."

"Aye."

Ethan nodded to him and turned back toward the castle. Shaw knew Ethan wouldn't breathe a word of his secret, and he wished he dared to trust Ethan with the whole truth. But it was out of the question.

Ethan saw everything as right or wrong.

What Shaw had done years ago was wrong.

So wrong that Ethan would never understand.

Nor would anyone else.

CHAPTER TWO

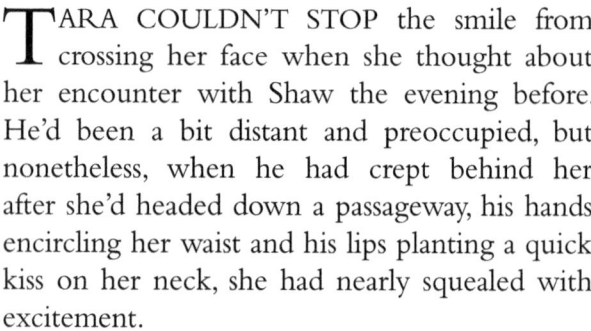

TARA COULDN'T STOP the smile from crossing her face when she thought about her encounter with Shaw the evening before. He'd been a bit distant and preoccupied, but nonetheless, when he had crept behind her after she'd headed down a passageway, his hands encircling her waist and his lips planting a quick kiss on her neck, she had nearly squealed with excitement.

Riley brought her back to the present morn and their outing across Black Isle when she asked, "Why are you smiling this morn? Thoughts of a long-haired Matheson with gray eyes and a beard dominating your mind?"

Tara laughed and pointed out, "They all have gray eyes."

"True. But they don't have beards like the one does. How about the only unattached Matheson?"

"I prefer to think Shaw is attached to me already." She fanned her eyelashes at her sister just as a loud boom echoed across the glade they were crossing. Both of their horses sidestepped at the roll of thunder.

Riley stared up at the sky. "That lightning bolt came out of nowhere."

"And so you think it will rain?" She wished to ask her if the bolt coming from an area close to the faerie glen was indicative of something important.

"Nay, I think it might mean something else is coming…"

Tara pulled her horse closer to her sister because she knew what she referred to. Sometimes, when she had her seer's visions or connected with the dead, odd things happened in the sky. She kept talking to keep her sister oriented, something Riley had asked all her family to do if she had a spell. "Shaw was oddly distant last night."

"He didn't look distant when he was nuzzling your neck," Riley drawled.

"But he was. His mind was on other things besides me," she declared, still watching her sister and not moving far away. She knew exactly how these things went, and she didn't want Riley to take a fall from her horse. "Should we stop?"

Riley didn't answer, instead staring straight ahead in a pose Tara didn't like.

Tara's heart jumped straight into her throat. It was too late to get her off her horse. Riley's head rolled back in that familiar way she had, so Tara slowed her horse and grabbed the reins of her sister's mount, stopping both their horses. Her sister was not fully present at that moment.

She waited for her sister's episode to run its course, holding both horses still until Riley could think again.

The sun was just past its highest point, and it peeked through the clouds often enough to warm them a wee bit. They were nearing the faerie glen on Black Isle, and her sister's episode told her one thing—the area was full of mystical properties, something her sister could always detect.

Her sister's head snapped back up, and she stared at Tara. "I had a session, didn't I?"

Tara nodded, handing the reins back to her sister. "I'm not surprised, given the stories I've heard about this part of Black Isle. I know not why it took me so long to bring you here. 'Tis a lovely area and there is some presence here, either in the waterfalls or the surrounding area. I knew it when I was here the first time, and every time I come back, it gets stronger. Your episode is proof I was right."

"I can feel the aura of the faeries, their power, their presence, their happiness, though I can also feel a disgruntled one or two. They have something to tell us." Riley's gaze scanned the area, her long dark curly hair waving in the wind behind her. Tara's sister was an unusual person, her spirit committed to nature and the unknown. She'd even been known in the past to connect with those who had passed on, those who still had a message for the living.

Those who had died too soon.

Tara smiled at her sister, so glad she was finally here on Black Isle. "Then we must move on. Give them the opportunity to say what they must. Can you continue or would you like to take a wee break?"

"How much farther to the faerie glen?"

"Just past that ridge." Tara gestured to the rise just ahead of them.

"Nay, I'll be fine."

They rode on, Tara leading the way, and a few minutes later, they came to the end of their path and a spot to tie their horses. Tara and Riley dismounted, looped their reins around a low tree branch, then Tara pointed through the trees to an open area that would lead them to the faerie glen, the soothing sound of cascading water calling to them.

Riley's face lit up in anticipation of meeting a faerie or two. Their aunt Avelina had the same sense, the same knowledge of the otherworld, as their mother called it. It was disconcerting to people encountering it for the first time, but Tara had grown up with her sister's abilities and welcomed her insights. She wondered what Riley would discover here.

They stepped through the line of trees and stopped. Tara always did when she came here, as if it were proper, as if she were seeking permission to enter this mystical area. In truth, the sight of the twin waterfall was so breathtakingly beautiful that it needed to be taken in slowly. Autumn was by far the best season to view it, the brilliant leaf colors around the blue of the falls and stream enrapturing.

The birch and oak trees decorated the land along the top of the waterfall, their graceful branches spreading to the sky but still allowing enough sun through to glint off the stream. The whisper of falling leaves echoed against the sound of the water hitting the rocks below.

The place was enchanting.

Riley reached for her hand and squeezed it, never turning to look at her, but striding forward, towing her sister behind her, drawn by some invisible power that only Riley understood. Even though Tara was the elder, Riley always took charge in mystical areas.

"Tara," she whispered. "There is so much here. So much history, so many legends." Her voice dropped as she freed her hand from Tara's only to clasp her own hands in front of her as they neared the water's edge. Riley closed her eyes and breathed deeply before whispering to the wind, "Come, tell me how I can help."

Tara knew that odd comment wasn't directed at her, so she kept her thoughts to herself while her gaze remained on her sister. Who was she talking with?

A rustle of branches off to the right caught her attention, so Tara tugged on Riley's sleeve. "Come. We must go now. I know not who could be coming. I know not whose land this is."

Riley waved her hand at her sister in dismissal, something Tara hated.

"Wait. Someone is coming to us, someone who has a story that needs to be told. I can sense it, Tara."

"How can you know that?" Tara asked, astounded at the strength of her sister's reaction to the glen.

"Because she told me," her sister said, tipping

her head toward the edge of the clearing. "Be patient. She is coming."

"Who is she?" But she didn't have to pester her sister any longer, because a white horse stepped out of the forest and into the clearing.

Riley held her hand up to her sister to indicate they shouldn't move at all. "Let her come to us." She held her fingers to her lips, so Tara kept her mouth closed and watched the animal in front of her, at times looking like a mirage. She pranced in a small circle, tossing her white mane proudly, casting a glance at Riley as she came closer, welcoming her. The proud beast's hooves looked to barely touch the ground as she glided across the grass. The animal let out two snorts in either greeting or excitement, the sound reminding them how large and strong she was, yet she was as graceful as a swan floating across water.

Was she floating? She circled the area two more times, her head held high on a broad neck and chest that rippled with power.

The horse stopped in front of them and stood as tall as one of her uncle's warhorses, its stance proud. Its gaze locked on Riley's in a way that sent a chill down Tara's spine. Up close, her eyes appeared violet, the color of a thistle in full blossom, but transparent.

It was as if one could see right through her eyes into her soul. Or was the horse looking into Riley's soul? That thought gave her shivers. Here she stood in a world she didn't comprehend, trusting her sister's judgment completely.

She opened her mouth to speak, but Riley

glared at her. "Not yet. Let her speak. She must trust us first."

Speak? What in all God's green grasses did that mean? Horses didn't talk. She bit her tongue and allowed Riley to manage the situation.

The horse tipped its head toward Riley, and a small protrusion appeared in the middle of its forehead, right between its eyes. A single horn, spiraling silver and straight as an arrow. Transfixed by the vision, Tara couldn't have spoken if she wished to. The horn grew a bit more, and the animal lifted its head, the movement drawing attention to a gold chain wrapped around the animal's body, looping around its neck, over its back, and down its legs.

"Are you still a maiden, Tara?" her sister whispered.

"Of course," she answered swiftly, a bit annoyed with the question. "What does…"

Her sister held her hand up to stop her. "The horn makes her a unicorn, though she was a horse when she lived. Unicorns prefer to be around maidens. A sign of their purity. How long have you been a unicorn?" she asked, patting the side of the animal's neck.

A unicorn? Of course she had heard of them, but she'd never seen one, nor heard of anyone who had. What did all this mean?

The horse stepped back and began to trot in a circle around the clearing again, the chains jingling while the white mane bounced with its movement. The horn, initially something odd and threatening, became something quite beautiful, giving the animal a regal look, as if it were the queen of the forest.

"Riley?" she whispered, watching the animal return to its original spot, then glancing back over its shoulder at Riley as if prompting her to follow.

Riley took one step forward but then stopped. "Lies from the past keep her locked in those chains. She needs to be set free, and she wants our help."

"I don't understand."

"She's locked in the otherworld waiting for someone to uncover the truth. She'll only be a unicorn while she waits. She has the power to heal others, if necessary, but 'tis only because she cannot leave this spot. Once the truth is revealed, she can move on." Riley took three more steps toward the white horse while Tara took two steps back.

"Be careful. She could impale you with that horn. What do the chains mean?"

"Unicorns are often depicted in chains, which represents how they are often imprisoned for different reasons, but this one's chains were forged by lies. She has been for several years, and she wishes to be free. Unicorns represent purity and innocence, so someone on Black Isle is struggling under the lies that have held them for a long time. The horse and the person, held by the same chains. She wishes for the truth to be revealed. Only then can she move on. She wishes for my help."

"How can we do that?"

The animal came closer to Riley, moving its head toward her. Tara nearly screamed. "Riley, be careful!"

The animal tipped its head so the horn was away from Riley and gently nuzzled Riley's hand with its muzzle. Riley spoke to her as if they carried on a conversation. "I understand, and I will do my best to release you from your bindings. It may take some time, but I promise to be persistent. You must be verra lonely."

The horse whinnied, stepped back, and shook its head, then stepped past Riley to Tara. She jumped back.

Riley followed and reached for her hand. "Don't, sister. She has something to tell you."

Tara held her breath and let her sister lead the horse to her.

"Hold out your hand," Riley urged.

Tara glared at her sister but did as she instructed. The white animal gently nuzzled her palm, feeling just as warm and soft as a flesh and blood pony's nose, then took a step closer and rested her head on Tara's shoulder. Tara froze, not daring to move, but she allowed Riley to take her hand and settle it on the horse's neck, her fingers resting on the soft hair there, and she stroked the animal.

She found it oddly soothing, more even than with her own horse. In fact, the unicorn was much warmer than her own, the heat spreading along her arm and into her neck, causing her to lift her own head. That brought her gaze to the marking on her ear. "You're not quite spotless, are you?" She touched the brown quarter-moon mark to see if she would react, but instead she stepped closer to Tara.

"Oh my," Riley whispered.

"What? What does this mean?"

"Hush," Riley whispered, as the unicorn stepped back and moved toward the trees again, the vision disappearing into a mirage, the white of her hair shimmering in the light as if it had never been there.

Tara stared after the animal, wondering what it all meant.

Riley turned to her with a wide smile on her face. "It means *you* can find the answer she needs."

"Me? Why me?"

"Probably because you've been on Black Isle longer than I have. Or it could also mean…"

"What?" Tara stared at her sister, afraid to hear the answer.

"Mayhap you belong on Black Isle."

CHAPTER THREE

STILL BOTHERED BY all that had happened last eve, Shaw stood on the shore of the bay with Ethan. His brother had suggested the walk, saying he'd had a thought about Shaw's problem overnight.

"What do you propose, Ethan? You have an idea?"

"I wish to pursue the person who leaves messages for Samuel." Ethan rarely used nicknames, and Sammy's full name struck Shaw's ear strangely.

"You think I haven't tried that?" He paced in a circle, glancing every once in a while at the dancing dolphins not far from them, their chatter echoing across the water. It was nearly supper time, and he hadn't seen Tara anywhere. Where had she gone?

"Tell me what you have tried in the past."

Shaw gathered his thoughts, clucking his tongue as he recalled the attempts he'd made over the years.

"That many different methods?" Ethan asked.

Shaw scowled, hated that his brother knew his ways so well. "I'm not counting, just thinking."

He glared at his brother, but stopped pacing when he drew close. "I tried watching the place after Sammy left the money, on two occasions, but the man never materialized. Once, I stayed well hidden for two days, and he still never showed. There's a place where Sammy leaves the coin and picks up the blackmailer's messages. He rarely deals with a person."

"Mayhap 'tis not a man."

"What?" Hell, but why hadn't that ever occurred to him. "A woman? I doubt it."

"Or another lad or a lass serving as a messenger. 'Twould not be difficult to watch from afar and send a child to retrieve or deliver something. Where exactly are the messages left?"

"He changes locations."

"How do you know when and where to pick them up?"

"Someone leaves a missive near the gate with specific instructions for each new location. We've tried to catch them, but we can't. Happens in the middle of the night." He ran his hand through his hair, then said to his brother, "Do you not see these gray hairs popping up on my head? These are from all the times I've tried to outsmart the bastard and failed."

"Any idea where he'll go next? Is there a pattern?"

"Nay, if I knew, I'd already be there." Sometimes he could get frustrated with Ethan's strict logic.

"Mayhap we need to go farther. Why not go to Inverness and see what we can uncover there? Someone might have heard or seen something—

not everyone stays on Black Isle, and they might be more talkative away from here. Word travels fast."

"Aye, could work. Will ye come with me? An extra pair of ears and your skill at observation would be welcome."

"Of course. Between the two of us, we should be able to uncover the truth."

"And Sammy?"

"Aye, that could be even better," Ethan said. "You know what they say about two being better than one…and three would help even more."

"I don't…what?"

"We can work better together than one person can alone." He gave Shaw an odd look, but he turned away when the sound of horses reached them. Shaw followed his gaze toward the main path, and he couldn't be more surprised to see Tara and Riley heading for the castle. With her sister visiting, he'd noticed they were quite close and did everything together, but he wished they would not go off just the two of them, after all that had happened on Black Isle lately.

His gaze fell on Tara and every thought in his mind melted, including the lecture he'd been forming in his mind, as if a hundred suns fell upon him. Tara greeted him with a beautiful smile, an expression he'd come to treasure over the months she'd been part of the Matheson household. With a word to Riley, she diverted them from the path back to the castle, and they headed straight toward Shaw and Ethan.

"Greetings to you both. 'Tis a most fine day, is it

not?" she asked. The front of her long brown hair was pulled back above her ears, joining the rest of her beautiful mane flowing freely down her back. He'd dreamed of her wearing naught but those long locks, the front covering her breasts with just the tips of her nipples peeking through…

"Shaw!" Ethan elbowed him.

"What?" he grumbled, but then changed his tune because Tara now gazed at him with such pleasure that it humbled him.

"You were supposed to be telling them why they should not be unescorted on the Isle. Never you mind. I'll do it," Ethan said. He turned to the women and beat Shaw to his lecture. "You lasses should not be out alone on Black Isle, after all that has transpired of late."

"I thought the villains were all caught," Riley said, looking from her sister to the two men.

"They were, but 'tis always good to be careful," Ethan said.

"Where are you coming from?" Shaw asked.

"We visited the faerie glen," Tara answered.

"Did you meet any faeries?" he asked with a chuckle.

Riley replied, "We did."

What the hell did one say to that declaration? Shaw felt like a wee laddie, and it wasn't just because of Riley's declaration about faeries. He glanced at Tara. How many times had he been around her and felt like his tongue was so thick with honey that it stuck to the roof of his mouth? He couldn't think of anything to say, so he blurted out the first words that came to his tongue.

"Ethan and I are going to Inverness. Mayhap you would like to travel with us."

"Inverness?" Tara said, her smile growing wider. "I would love to go. May we go shopping through the vendor stalls? We must go on market day."

Shaw nodded in agreement. "Every day is market day in Inverness," he said. "If you've no plans for the morrow, we can leave in the morn. I have a surprise for you."

"You do? I love surprises. Is Jennet going along, Ethan?"

"When I ask her, I think she might consider traveling with us. I'll speak to her this eve."

Tara pulled on the reins of her horse. "Never mind. I'll go ask now. Thank you for the invitation. I promise we'll take guards with us on our next exploration."

And the two were gone.

"You have developed strong feelings for Tara," Ethan said. Anyone else would have teased him about it, but Ethan spoke it as a mere statement of fact.

"I think so, but I can't..."

"Just because you are being blackmailed doesn't mean you cannot pursue a lass. And what do you plan to do with them in Inverness while we're hunting for your blackmailer?"

Shaw scowled. "I'll think of something. Surely it cannot be so difficult." Shaw started pacing again while his brother stood and watched. Faithful, loyal Ethan. He never failed his family. Always there, and they knew exactly what to expect of him. While Shaw changed with the wind and

Marcas kept most of his thoughts to himself, they always knew how Ethan felt about an issue. He wore his plaid the same way every day, no pleat out of place, the end tossed over his shoulder resting precisely the same length and width.

How could he explain that he just wished to be with Tara away from here? Away from the watching eyes and wagging tongues. Ethan couldn't understand how many times Shaw felt like evil eyes were tracking him, noting his every move and word. He'd never understand that because Shaw had no idea who was blackmailing him, he was suspicious of everyone.

He wanted to be with Tara alone. Not to be improper but to be able to speak freely.

To not always be looking over his shoulder.

"You've already promised her shopping. And what will that surprise be? Do you even know? You should think of something special. Lasses like to feel special and all dressed up," Ethan said, scratching his chin. That was something he did when he was trying to come up with suggestions, a difficult task for him at times.

Other people scratched their heads, Ethan scratched his chin.

Shaw was about to curse, thinking he'd made a huge mistake promising Tara a surprise. Then he stopped, his mind going to his parents. "Ethan, do you recall when Papa took Mama to the dressmaker?"

"Aye, Mama spoke of it for many moons."

"'Tis where I'll take Tara."

Ethan gave him a skeptical look. "I'm sure

you're aware of the obvious. Buying a gown in Inverness will be quite expensive."

"I have enough." Shaw did a quick calculation in his brain. While the four siblings had inherited coin after the deaths of their parents, he'd had to spend more than he wished on the blackmailer.

"You should not squander your coin. Papa meant for it to be used for your marriage and your bairns." Again Ethan seemed to know exactly what he was thinking. Sometimes his insight was eerie. Could he read minds and had kept the ability a secret all this time?

Nay, Ethan did not keep secrets, especially when asked outright. And Shaw was certain he himself had asked his brother if he could read minds many times, in jest or wonderment.

"This could be an investment in my upcoming marriage, if Tara agrees to marry me eventually." Ethan said nothing, seemingly lost in thought. Shaw hazarded a guess about what was on his mind. "You could buy a dress for Jennet."

Ethan's gaze narrowed, telling Shaw he'd guessed correctly. "Jennet is not taken by material things. She makes her own clothing, not trusting others to have the stitches tight enough."

Shaw laughed. "You two deserve each other."

"I don't understand the meaning of that statement, though I do agree that Jennet and I make a perfect pair."

"Never mind. I must get ready for the morrow." Shaw began to walk away, but his brother stopped him.

"Shaw, we must tell Marcas about the blackmail."

Shaw groaned. "Ethan, I don't wish to bring Marcas into it. He has enough to worry about as newly made laird and newly married at the same time."

"'Tis the rule. We must tell him."

Shaw let out a huge sigh, because he knew once Ethan latched onto an idea that was caused by a rule, he'd not let go. "Fine. We'll tell him, but not until later this eve. He's been busy going over ledgers and accounts, taking stock of inventory for winter. We need not bother him right this moment. Promise me, Ethan."

"I promise, but only until later."

"Or the morrow. I'll see how he is first. And I'll tell him in my own way. 'Tis my tale to tell, not yours."

"Agreed."

How he prayed that was enough to pacify his brother, because he had no plan to tell Marcas until they returned from Inverness.

He needed more information and a plan to solve the difficulty or Marcas would never be satisfied with only half the tale. He'd make him tell all, and he couldn't do it.

The truth was too shameful.

CHAPTER FOUR

TARA FLEW INTO the great hall, nearly squealing with glee, but she stopped when she saw how many people were there. The men were all seated and enjoying their evening meal, many with their wives.

She glanced over her shoulder at her sister. "Are we that late?"

Riley shrugged her shoulders. "The sun is dropping, so I suppose Ethan had a good point about not being about on our own. I'm starving. I'm going to our chamber to freshen up, then I'll meet you back here for our meal."

Tara nodded, then crossed the hall to Brigid, who sat near the fire with her back to the room. Nonie, the Matheson housekeeper who had been with them forever and now helped Brigid, had fashioned a partition so they could continue to dress the wee ones near the hearth where it was the warmest without everyone watching. Tara stuck her head around the partition.

"Might I have a quick word while I wait for Riley?"

Brigid and Jennet both looked up and greeted

her, Brigid nodding while Jennet waved her inside the small area. "Come join us."

"Greetings, Auntie Tara," Kara said, the three-year-old giving her a wide grin. Tiernay, at just over a year, yawned before grinning at her.

"Greetings, my sweet Kara." She exchanged a few more words with the little one, then turned to her cousins. "Jennet, Ethan and Shaw are going to Inverness, and Shaw has invited me. Will you come, too? Ethan said you're welcome to join us."

"Are you certain he's going? He prefers to stay here. Was it Shaw's idea?"

"Shaw invited me, but they seemed to have settled the trip between them before we joined their conversation," she said, glancing back outside of the partition to see if she saw Ethan or Shaw anywhere. "Ethan said he would invite you to go with us. Brigid, will you come with us?"

Kara set her tiny palm and placed it on Brigid's cheek, turning her face away from Tara's. "Nay, my new mama would prefer to stay here with us."

Kara had been stolen away a few months ago, tied in the forest alone before Brigid's mother had found her and brought her home. Ever since then, she preferred not to leave Matheson land, and she didn't wish her mother or father to leave either.

Brigid said, "Aye, I'd prefer to stay with you, my sweet." She kissed Kara's cheek, and the wee lass giggled with pleasure. She turned back to Tara, "'Tis best for now, but you go and have fun. Find us some pretty new ribbons. Or some new fabric in a pretty shade of green."

Tara looked to Jennet. "Will you come along?"

"It sounds fun. I've always wished to travel to Inverness to see more of the burgh and the harbor where all the ships come in. Even though we can see some across the water from here, 'tis not the same."

"Well, Shaw promised a surprise for me, so I cannot wait to go. We're going on the morrow, but I know no more than that."

Brigid lifted Tiernay and said, "You have fun. It's time for me to put the bairns to bed, tell them a story or two. You, Jennet, and Riley need to eat. Jinny's stew was delicious this eve. Fresh vegetables. When I return, mayhap we can enjoy a jar of wine together."

"I am hungry, and it smells wonderful." She made her way to an empty trestle table, Jennet following her. A moment later, Riley joined them. Edda brought out two steaming bowls of stew and went back for the third.

After Edda left, Jennet asked, "How was your visit to the faerie glen?"

"It was most interesting," she replied, looking over her shoulder to see if it was safe to speak. Being honest could set many tongues wagging, but the place was emptying out and their area was deserted. "A white horse visited us, and it turned into a unicorn right in front of us." She couldn't stop the excitement in her voice over the issue. She would never tell her Grant cousins about the magical beast. Only Aunt Avelina's family would believe her. "I still have trouble believing it truly happened. I think it was a mirage. Riley said it was an unsettled spirit trapped by lies and it needs the truth to be told."

Riley nodded. "The unicorn spoke of a lie that was told years ago, and we must uncover what it is. We must try to find the truth—she's charged us with the task."

"Do you believe all that, Tara?" Jennet asked. "Sometimes I believe faeries and otherworldly creatures are possible, and other times I think it to be most childish."

"We saw this horse with our own eyes, and the horn was as real as the rest of it, so aye, I do believe it. I cannot explain it, but I think there's a truth to be uncovered on Black Isle." Tara stirred the thick soup, finding a piece of carrot to try first.

"Where will you start?" Jennet asked, taking another sip of her own stew.

Tara and Riley looked at each other for a moment, pausing, but then Riley said, "'Tis Tara's job. The unicorn said so."

"The animal spoke?" Jennet persisted.

"Nay, not out loud. 'Tis hard to explain, but I just know. The horse was more interested in Tara than me, yet I am the link between the two worlds. Stepping past me to get to Tara was important."

Jennet asked, "So how do you plan to go about this? Would Marcas or his brothers know? What part of Black Isle is involved?"

"We don't know anything specific, so I guess we'll just start asking the members of Clan Matheson."

Jennet considered that for a moment. "Please don't start asking questions yet. With all this clan has been through, you could be stirring up old wounds that don't need to be opened. Why not let it go for now?"

Riley shook her head emphatically. "Nay, we cannot ignore this unicorn. She was in chains and longs to be set free. We'll certainly go about it carefully, but there's no need to wait. Mayhap finding this truth will finally help the clan truly recover. We could start just by gathering stories from some of the clan's oldest members—they've been here the longest."

"I agree," Tara said, cutting in. "I believe it to be important, but I also agree with Jennet. We should wait a bit until we start asking questions on Black Isle. The trip to Inverness is the morrow. Mayhap we can ask a few questions there. Whatever it was could have happened to another clan or even off Black Isle entirely. 'Tis just that the horse sensed someone nearby who had the power to hear its request for help. So the trip to Inverness is an opportunity we shouldn't miss. Jennet, if you come along, you could help listen to the old stories and the gossip about grudges and clan feuds."

Jennet chuckled, something she didn't do often. "I guess you just gave me a good reason to go to Inverness. I think I'll be requesting to travel with you." She had a small smirk on her face that Tara didn't really trust.

"Why do you like this idea so much, cousin?"

Tara asked.

"Because I think we could be about to uncover something big. And this time, I wish to hear all. And I wish to see those chains gone from the poor beast."

Tara said, "Then I'm sure we'll find the truth on the morrow. Ethan recalls everything that has happened on Black Isle. I expect he can help us uncover the truth and free that beautiful horse."

"I think you are correct, Tara. Ethan recalls everything as if it happened a day ago. If anyone has the answer, it will be him. Whoever is lying will be uncovered."

Something about that statement caught Tara wrong, but it was no more than a feeling, some remnant of the sensation she'd had upon seeing the unicorn's chains.

Riley must have sensed the change in her. She whispered, "What is it?"

"I'm not sure. It's just…" Tara wished the thought hadn't entered her mind. "What if the reason the horse came to me is because I'm closer to the person who knows about what happened?"

Ethan entered, so Jennet strode over to greet him. Tara watched them speaking together, only half paying attention.

"I suppose 'tis possible," said Riley. "Why does that thought bother you?"

Tara shrugged and forced a small smile onto her face. "No reason."

If her sister saw through her lie, she didn't mention it, instead reaching for a piece of bread from the basket on the table. But the thought persisted.

What if the person who had lied was Shaw?

CHAPTER FIVE

THE NEXT DAY, Ethan and Jennet, Tara and Shaw, along with four guards, arrived in Inverness at midday, grateful the mist had finally lifted so they could move about the burgh without being drenched. Because of the weather, they hadn't talked much on the journey, instead huddling inside their mantles to stay warm and keep off the chill of the autumn damp.

To Tara's surprise, Riley had stayed behind, telling the others she didn't feel well. But Tara knew better. "I think you'll learn more without me around," Riley had confided to her sister.

Tara couldn't disagree.

Ethan said, "I need food. Let's go to the inn first. Then we can shop the vendors."

"That sounds fine," Tara said. She could hardly wait for her surprise, but she forced herself to tamp down her excitement.

To her surprise, Shaw said, "Have a lovely meal with Jennet, Ethan. I'm taking Tara for her surprise."

Tara said nothing, just grinned from ear to ear as they said their goodbyes. She loved to simply watch Shaw, especially outside. While his long brown hair was nearly the same color as his brothers', his hair had strands of dark red when the sun hit it just right. He kept it long, but unlike Ethan, who kept every stand in place, Shaw's sometimes went every which way, truly an indication that things other than neatness were more important to him. And his beard had even more red strands in it. She had to admit she was quite fascinated by his beard.

When he turned toward her and gave her a wide smile, his gaze falling on her, her heart fluttered with happiness. She could see the joy in his steel-gray eyes, and in that moment, she realized she hadn't seen that joy lately.

Something was bothering Shaw, and she vowed to uncover what it was.

Ethan gave instructions to the four guards who'd come with them while Shaw led her down a side street and to a building with a sign on the door unlike anything she'd ever seen—"Tailor."

She hadn't known it was possible to visit a place that focused on women's gowns. Nearly squealing with delight, she stepped inside, Shaw taking her hand as if that small move would protect her from everything.

She liked it.

They paused inside, allowing their eyes to adjust to the dimness, though the shop owner came forward carrying a large tallow candle. "May I be of assistance to you?"

"Aye," Shaw said. "We are here to purchase a gown for my companion. Have you something that might fit her? We're only in town for a short time."

Tara thought she would explode with excitement. The shopkeeper led them into the back of the shop, through two other chambers, one full of fabrics and trims, the other with accessories such as slippers and shawls. She even saw some accessories for men. But the last room was the best of all. She gasped as she took in the sight.

The chamber was busy with seamstresses working on different gowns, some already on the forms they used to hold the gown up for view. "This is where we make our most elegant gowns. I'm sorry to say we have no gowns ready to purchase. Each gown is carefully crafted to fit the owner's measurements, so what we make for another would hardly fit you. But if you like, I'd be happy to take your measurements and we can choose the fabric. Then we could have it ready in a fortnight or so. Would that work for you?"

Tara glanced around at the women hard at work, metal pins everywhere. The gowns were at various stages of completion and all different, some in styles she'd never seen before. A corner of the room had been partitioned off, a curtain across the opening.

The man played with the scissors hanging from his tool belt. She looked at Shaw who looked nearly as disappointed as she did. He said, "Forgive us for taking up your time. We cannot return."

"I suggest you check the vendor's marketplace. You can find some decent pieces there." He gave them a small bow. "I hope you'll return when you have more time. 'Twould be my pleasure to design a gown for your lady."

Tara asked, "Are we permitted to look at the fabric choices you have? I would consider purchasing some to take home with me."

"Aye. Much of our material is already spoken for, but if you see something you like, please ask. I'll be in the back."

Once he left, Shaw rubbed his beard, the look on his face showing his vulnerability. He said, "Please forgive me. I thought he would have a couple already completed. I was hopeful, though Marcas told me it wouldn't be so."

"'Tis fine, Shaw. I would like to look around. Just coming here is a delight. All these colors! And I'll remember these designs for later and perhaps attempt to replicate them." She stroked a fine length of lace but knew it would be wasted on her day-to-day wear.

Shaw cursed under his breath. "I failed you, lass."

"Nay, you did not. I came to spend time with you. 'Tis what matters most. I have all the clothing I need." She was a healer so most of her clothes were working clothes and couldn't be so fine she'd mind stains and tears. She had two gowns with her, but none that were new.

They were about to leave when the proprietor called out to them. "Excuse me, but I do have one gown that was rejected by the husband after the wife ordered it. The color is a rich purple, and with your lovely hair color, it would be stunning on you." The man stood back, rubbing his chin as he looked Tara up and down, judging her size and her height. "I think it would fit you near perfectly, and if not, it would only require a wee bit of altering. Would you like to see it?"

Tara looked at Shaw and she could feel the smile on her face. "Oh, Shaw, do we have the time?"

"Absolutely. I'd love to see you try it on, that is, if you like the color."

The shopkeeper called to one of the women, and she brought out a beautiful gown with a few ruffles and a deeply brocaded bodice. "Do you like the color, my lady?"

"Aye, it is lovely."

The owner said, "If you would like to try it on, please come this way, and Beatrice will assist you. We have an alcove for changing right over here."

Shaw looked to her, arching his brow in question.

"I'll try it on if you do not mind waiting." She prayed he'd allow her this luxury.

"Of course," he said with a smile.

The shopkeeper pointed to a chair where Shaw could sit, then led her to the curtained alcove. While the woman helped her change, she could hear Shaw and the shopkeeper's conversation.

"You could choose material to take along home with you, my lord. Or various ribbons or a bodice. Ladies love wee gifts as a surprise. Perhaps tuck some away for a special occasion. This green fabric would be a good choice—there are many choices of ribbons to match. And some satin for the edges."

"I think the lady would choose what she prefers better than I would. I look forward to seeing her in the gown you brought out. I was hoping to find a gown so lovely for her."

Tara had never experienced anything that pleased her more. As she tried on the gown, the assistant adjusted it this way and that, stuck a few pins in it to fit it just right.

"I can take a tuck in here, perhaps raise the hem, but with new slippers, you might be fine." The gown made her feel like a true princess in a royal castle, and she knew she could never accept such an extravagant gift. The bodice, woven with gold thread, practically glowed. It was too dear a thing, especially with no understanding between Shaw and herself. They'd not even talked of courting. But she still wanted to see his reaction to seeing her in the gown.

She stepped out to get Shaw's opinion, and it was exactly as she hoped, judging by the way his mouth fell open. He loved it. "Tara…" He gave his head a little shake. "Aye, you're truly a queen. The color is glorious on you. Do you like it?"

"I do, but she said she would have to make alterations."

"Sir, let us converse while the lady gets dressed."

"Of course."

The two stepped out of the chamber while Tara switched back into the well-worn gown she'd come in. She loved the purple gown, but she had no idea how much it cost or how long it would take to make all the alterations.

When she stepped out of the changing area, the shopkeeper had returned, a smile on his face. He picked up the gown and said, "Your husband is pleased with the gown, but it does need numerous alterations. Sadly, we cannot complete them for you while you are in town."

From the look on Shaw's face, Tara suspected that cost was also a factor. Inverness was not so far that the gown could not be fetched or picked up by someone passing between Black Isle and the Grant or Ramsay lands, or even her own home. "I feared as much. Thank you for allowing me to try it on. It was a pleasure to wear it even for just a few moments."

Shaw took her hand in his and gave it a little squeeze. "We shall find something you love from one of the vendor's stalls."

The look of disappointment on his face tugged at her heartstrings. "Nay, I need naught. I am here for your company and to enjoy Inverness. Mayhap we could take a stroll down to the port. See the ships coming in from Europe."

"I'd like that. Someday, we'll return and order a beautiful gown designed just for you."

"Mayhap someday." She had to admit that she had no place to wear anything so precious. But she had enjoyed the trip into a world she'd not seen before.

This had been more fun than she could have guessed.

CHAPTER SIX

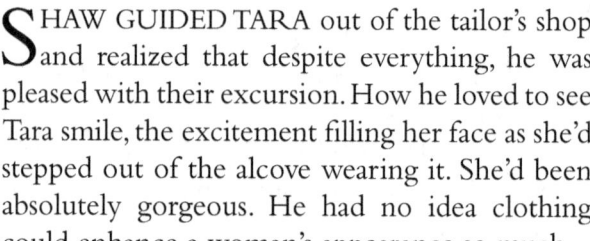

SHAW GUIDED TARA out of the tailor's shop and realized that despite everything, he was pleased with their excursion. How he loved to see Tara smile, the excitement filling her face as she'd stepped out of the alcove wearing it. She'd been absolutely gorgeous. He had no idea clothing could enhance a woman's appearance so much.

But he'd learned two things that were very important. First, Tara Cameron was a woman of character. She didn't seem disappointed by the fact that he hadn't been able to buy her the dress. And he was certain she understood the real reason they'd had to leave without it. The understanding on her face had told him that. On the contrary, she'd acted thrilled over just the chance to try on such a beautiful gown. How he wished he could have indulged her every wish.

Marcas's late wife Freda would not have acted that way. He would have received only tears and pouting from her. He would never wish her harm, but neither could he mourn her death from the curse very much. Marcas had been blessed by meeting Brigid, and he'd never seen his brother happier. Indeed, Marcas and Brigid's match had lifted the spirits of the whole clan.

The second thing he'd learned was perhaps his strongest motivation for finding the blasted blackmailer. If he hadn't given the bastard so much coin over the years, he would have had the funds to purchase that gown and plenty left over. How he would have loved to gift Tara with that extravagant outfit, including a pair of matching slippers. He'd briefly thought of asking Ethan for the coin. Ethan would have given it to him without a second thought. He was generous to a fault. But Shaw wouldn't ask. This situation was his fault. His doing. The quickly hidden disappointment in Tara's face was his fault. Nay— the blackmailer's fault.

This had to stop.

It had been wonderful to step away from all his problems for a few hours. But soon, he'd have to return to them and start asking questions in the burgh. Questions of his own.

But not yet.

On their way to meet Ethan and Jennet, they indeed paused at a few stalls along the street. Tara chose a few lengths of ribbon, saying she'd promised them to Brigid, and Shaw found toys for Tiernay and Kara. And when Tara lingered over skeins of the softest fawn-colored wool, he'd bought the lot for her without a second thought.

"Winter's on the way," he said. "And when you wear a mantle made of this, perhaps you'll feel my arms around you, warming you."

She'd blushed and ducked her head, but not

quick enough to hide her smile.

When they finally reached the inn, Shaw was surprised to find Ethan and Jennet still eating in a side chamber. Bowls of stew—it smelled like lamb—and a platter of fruit and cheese sat before them.

It was no surprise Ethan had asked for a table away from the main dining room. The cacophony of multiple different conversations made it difficult for him to sit still.

"This is a comfortable area, Ethan." Then he motioned to the innkeeper. "We'll have the same as our friends."

He held a chair for Tara, then sat down himself, and a moment later had their own meals. The serving lasses here dressed more neatly than in many establishments, and he guessed that was why Ethan preferred this inn over the others.

"So what was your surprise?" Jennet asked as soon as they were alone.

"Oh, Jennet, you should have seen it! I tried on a lovely purple gown at the tailor. The woman who ordered it didn't take it, so it was already completed. The bodice was fitted, and the ribbons were dark gold and royal purple.

"Where is it?" Jennet asked.

"It did not fit me exactly right and would have taken too long to alter, so we decided to leave it. But it was such a fun experience. You should have seen all the fabrics he had. Fabrics and ribbons, slippers, shawls, lace, so many items. It was such fun. No wonder Mama liked to travel to Edinburgh for fabrics. I was never interested before, but now I think I'd go with her. We bought a few things from the vendors' stalls on the way back, though, including some beautifully soft wool and the ribbons Brigid asked for."

"My mother and Aunt Gwyneth both love to go as well. Aunt Gwyneth insists she must feel the weave of the wool to make the perfect pair of leggings with the right amount of give. I never thought there were so many varieties," Jennet said.

"I would not like so many choices, but our mama loved to come here at least once a year, though Papa often complained about the cost." Ethan looked at Shaw. "Was it overly expensive?"

"The gowns were priced rather high. I didn't have enough coin," Shaw answered sheepishly. "But they didn't have a gown ready to take anyway."

"I don't know how to thank you, Shaw, for taking me there," Tara whispered, blushing a touch. "It was a new experience, and I enjoyed it. I don't need a gown that fine anyway."

"I just need more coin."

"I think we can fix that," Ethan said, staring at Shaw.

"Not something I care to discuss now," Shaw said.

"Why not?" Ethan asked.

"Never mind," Jennet said. "We have a question for you."

Glad for the change in topic, Shaw bit into a chunk of bread, chewed, and said, "Please, anything. I'll answer in between bites."

Jennet nodded at Tara.

Tara set her spoon down and said, "Riley and I met an odd creature in the faerie glen near Rosemarkie yesterday."

Ethan asked, "What kind of creature?"

"At first, it appeared to be a horse, but then it sprouted a horn, like a unicorn's." Tara glanced at Shaw.

Shaw had heard others speak of unicorns, but he'd never seen one, nor was he sure he believed in them. Many did.

Ethan spoke right up, his interest in the subject clear. "Ah, the unicorn. The animal William used in his royal coat of arms. Mythological but 'tis known to be strong, wild and untamed, a beautiful creature that can only be humbled by a maiden. Said to be the symbol of purity and innocence. Some don't believe in the beast, but others swear they've seen them in the forest. You saw one?"

"Aye, she was quite beautiful. And she was bound by a chain."

"Was the chain golden?" Jennet asked.

"Aye. How did you know?" Tara gave Jennet a look of admiration.

Shaw was amazed at the breadth of Jennet's and Ethan's knowledge, often shocked by their combined comments.

"'Tis part of the myth," Ethan said. "No one is certain what it represents. And the horn is supposed to have healing properties, so 'tis most appropriate that it appeared to one of our healers. What think you of it, Tara? And what did Riley think?" He held Jennet close, leaning in to kiss her cheek at one point.

"Riley has demonstrated powers of a seer in the past, and even more importantly, she has been able to communicate with the dead in rare situations. We think the unicorn brought a message from some spirit—horse or human—whose memory is sullied by lies."

Shaw's belly tied into a knot. Thankfully, Ethan was being persistent with his questions, so he did not need to respond, but he had a bad feeling about this whole situation.

Tara continued, "She believes the unicorn is telling us that there was a lie told on Black Isle or somewhere close, and the unicorn is chained because of that lie. If the lie is uncovered, the unicorn will be set free by the truth."

Shaw choked on the sip of mead he'd just taken. What the hell was happening here? He forced himself to be calm, reminding himself that even Ethan knew nothing about the true circumstances behind the blackmail, so only he would notice any correlation to his situation. No one else would have reason to think it related to him.

Well, nearly no one. Clearly someone knew his secret, or there would be no blackmail.

"Shaw, are you all right?" Jennet asked, the concern on her face evident.

"Do either of you know of any situation that would have happened in the past few years that would have involved a horse? Anything at all?" Tara asked.

Shaw thanked the Lord above that he hadn't

told Ethan anything specific, or he'd be spilling it all now. No, he realized—he couldn't tell Ethan every detail.

He'd managed to get away that morning without having to tell Marcas anything either. Tiernay was sick, so Marcas was tending to his son, unable to visit with anyone. Shaw had convinced Ethan that Marcas's son was more urgent than his situation, which had been going on for years.

"I supposed another sennight will not matter," Ethan had said, and Shaw had thought he had a reprieve. He'd hoped to hear about someone who came by coin too easily in Inverness, but that could only happen if he actually talked to the locals and listened for gossip. A dress shop and a private room for their midday meal were not the best places to gather information of that sort.

Blast it, now there was a unicorn and a woman who could communicate with the dead.

Shaw had to ask one question. He hoped the answer would calm his quivering insides.

"What color was the unicorn?" he asked, hoping the shakiness in his voice was well hidden.

"White," Tara replied.

Ethan added, "Most unicorns are white, so 'tis nothing revealing at all about the incident."

Shaw let out the breath he'd been holding.

Tara frowned, then said, "Oh, and one other thing. It had a brown mark in the shape of a quarter moon under its right ear."

If Shaw had been standing, he'd have dropped to the floor.

He knew that horse.

CHAPTER SEVEN

TARA DIDN'T KNOW what to make of Shaw's reaction. He had turned paler than a snowflake in winter, but she didn't comment. He'd also changed the subject immediately, and she'd gone along with it.

All had been quiet for the rest of the meal. Afterward, with a couple of hours remaining before dusk, they decided to go in search of beautiful views. Tara and Shaw strolled down the path that led to the water of Beauly Firth, while Jennet and Ethan strolled through the market. They were to spend the night, Jennet and Tara sharing a bedchamber while the men slept on the floor in the passageway.

Tara thought it ridiculous, but Jennet was quick to say her father had done so before, and Ethan believed it to be the proper way to protect an unmarried woman in an inn. He'd assign the guards a post that they would take in turns, but while Shaw would have loved a night to hold Tara in his arms, he knew their upbringing would never allow Ethan to accept it. Their mother had drummed the idea of protecting lasses' reputations into their head. Ethan would never forget it either.

They strolled for a while without chatting, enjoying the peacefulness of the water and the evening. Their easy companionship made her feel special.

"'Tis so beautiful here."

Shaw took her hand in his. "Your hand is chilled. Are you cold, lass?"

"A wee bit." She tugged on her collar around her neck. "'Tis just the wind coming across the firth." When they came down a small hill, her gaze fell on the water as the sun dropped, the reflection sparkling golden. "'Tis Black Isle, nay?" She pointed across the river.

"Aye," he said, then he pointed down the river. "'Tis our bay across there, and Eddirdale Castle sits up a wee bit on the hill."

"'Tis a lovely view, Shaw. Many thanks for bringing me here. And for our visit to the tailor." And before she could say another word, his lips descended to hers, a soft kiss, one that made her want for more.

She slanted her head and parted her lips for him, one hand going to the back of his neck to run her fingers through his long locks. How she wished for this relationship to grow, even though she didn't know if her parents would support a marriage with such a distant clan.

He pulled back and whispered, "Tara, my feelings for you grow stronger every day. I wish we could spend more time together."

"I grow more intrigued by you too. Will you

just kiss me again while we have no worry of busybodies observing us?"

He chuckled, then complied, his tongue delving inside her mouth and his arms settling around her back, tugging her closer. She liked being so close to him. The cold disappeared, and her body heated up in private places, making her squirm for some kind of release, but their location didn't lend itself to the exploration she would prefer. His beard brushed against her skin in spots, but it didn't hurt. In fact, she liked his beard.

Their tongues dueled until she could hear his breathing speed up, telling her he liked their mating as much as she did. She would have to encourage him more often. He tasted of the baked apple he'd just eaten, and she wished to touch his bare skin. How she would love to hold her hands against his bare chest, discover his secrets, like how much chest hair he had and if he bore any scars.

"Shaw! Tara!" The voice ended their interlude. Jennet approached, Ethan behind her. "Sorry for the interruption but Ethan found something out for you."

Tara pulled back, but Shaw kept one arm around her, holding her close. She relished his embrace. He made her feel special, and she was glad he wasn't ashamed of their relationship. "About what, Ethan?"

"About whoever is blackmailing you, Shaw," he replied, coming even with Jennet and taking her hand in his.

"Blackmailing you? Truly?" Tara asked, staring

at Shaw, seeing the concern etched in his face. Could this be why he paled earlier? "How could anyone blackmail someone like you? You're a good and honorable man."

"Ethan, you were supposed to keep this between the two of us."

"So I was, but you also wished to gather information. 'Twas hard to do without explaining to Jennet. And once Marcas is told, Brigid will know, then Jennet and Tara, and it will travel. I saw little reason to hide it."

"True," Shaw said, looking from Jennet to Tara. "Please, 'tis not for general knowledge. I know you'll not spread the information."

"Why are you being blackmailed?" Jennet asked bluntly. "Blackmail suggests a villainous side to you, and I don't notice it."

"'Tis something that happened long ago, and the event doesn't matter. But I wish to end this extortion. It's been going on for too long. What did you learn, Ethan?"

Ethan lowered his voice as a few other people out enjoying the evening approached along the path, though they did not seem the least bit interested in them. "We passed an unsavory tavern known for gambling, and I overheard someone speaking of blackmail, so I left Jennet and two of the guards near the kirk so I could pursue the issue. I found out that one of the people known to use blackmail and accept bribes is one of the sheriffs. He loses all his money at cards and dice, but a sennight later, he's flush with coin. All in the tavern know he comes by it dishonestly."

Shaw frowned, and Tara's entire being wished to question him until he told her all. He was clearly upset by his circumstances, yet he did not deny or explain the blackmail. She'd heard of issues with the sheriffs. If she thought hard enough, she might be able to tell them exactly which sheriff she'd heard troubling stories about.

She gasped when it came to her. She couldn't believe any of them had forgotten. "The sheriff of Cromarty! He locked up Padraig because Donald MacKinnie paid him to do so. Gisela told us about him." Tara said. "Surely such a man might include blackmail among his crimes."

"Aye," Ethan said. "That's him. He's said to be good friends with the chief of Clan MacKinnie, Fearchar. MacKinnie has been around for a long time and has many connections. We saw how many warriors he was able to bring in for the battle over Gisela's marriage to his son."

Donald, Fearchar's younger son, had died during that battle, and some thought both his turn toward evil and his death were caused by a growth in his head. Tara thought it likely, from Brigid's description of his actions and the changes in him. Or perhaps the MacKinnies were dangerous by nature. Shaw didn't speak, and if Tara were to guess, she'd say his mind was racing at this connection between his situation and Gisela's.

"I suppose," she said slowly, not sure how Shaw would react, "we need to know if the sheriff could have been a part of the situation behind the blackmail." She wouldn't push him to tell the story, but sometime when they were alone, she'd ask again. What could have happened in his past that could warrant blackmailing? "Shaw, whatever it is, it cannot be that serious. You are a trustworthy, respectable man. Mayhap whatever the issue is, it isn't as bad as you think it is. We could help you."

Shaw kissed her cheek and said, "Your faith in me is appreciated, but I'm not ready to share the entire situation. 'Tis too long a tale to bother with now. Besides, this journey was supposed to be enjoyable, not a time to examine my character."

She had to agree with him on that point. While she loved to be this close to him, she couldn't help but wonder about a secret so troubling. Was it possible she was blind to his faults? Did he have a history she needed to know about before they continued their relationship?

She knew what her sire, Aedan Cameron, would say. *Aye, my girl. Ye must be sure of him before you give your pledge.*

"Did you learn anything else, Ethan?" Shaw asked.

"Nay, though I asked several others."

Shaw nodded, a look of defeat on his face. Tara decided to ease Shaw's discomfort. He wouldn't speak more of the blackmail anyway, so she'd change the subject. After all, she'd promised Riley she would see what she could learn from the brothers.

"I'd like to ask our own mysterious question as long as we are on odd topics."

Ethan nodded. "Feel free to ask anything you

wish. We'll help if we can."

She could almost sense the tension drain out of Shaw's body when she changed the subject. This was a good time to discuss the faerie glen. "You know my sister thinks the unicorn we saw is chained because of something that happened on Black Isle in the past. Was there any situation where a series of hurtful lies would have been told? Something that could cause someone a great deal of pain? I think it's likely the lies haven't been uncovered yet, or the unicorn would not still be trapped."

Shaw looked quickly to Ethan, who said, "Donald MacKinnie told many lies, but that wasn't long ago, and you already know of those events. And you know of the other lies that were all told since our clan was cursed. I'll have to think on what could have taken place before that. Naught stands out to me, but I'm sure there have been many lies told, and many never corrected. Finding the one lie that could have entrapped your unicorn could prove to be quite a challenge in these parts."

"I would think it would be over a major event, do you not agree, Jennet? Maybe someone dying or cattle stealing or something that might have caused a battle or clan feud."

Shaw shook his head. "We've not had much experience with battles, except for the one with the MacKinnies—and there's no hidden lies there. Black Isle is a small community, and the clans have many ties connecting us. Harm to one is harm to many. Perhaps the horse is referring to something that took place on the mainland, not Black Isle. I would search there. Perhaps 'tis why she came to you, Tara, since you're not from the Isle. We can ask about feuds and battles around Inverness and further away at the inn. They would know better than we would."

Jennet added, "Do not forget the situation with our cousins several years ago when bairns were being stolen and sold. Connor, Gregor, and Gavin were all in Inverness and caught someone trying to ship bairns in crates. Sending them across the water to Europe for coin."

"They were caught, though, aye? I do recall our sire mentioning this, but that was a long time ago." Ethan scratched his jaw. "That situation has been totally resolved to my knowledge."

"I'll give it some more thought," Shaw said, giving Tara a quick rub across her back. "But you should tell your horse about that. That could verra well be the answer to your mystery. I think 'tis time to head back to the inn. The sun has nearly dropped, bringing cold along with the darkness."

A shiver traveled down Tara's back, but oddly enough, it wasn't caused by the weather.

It came from Shaw; she was quite certain he was lying about her unicorn's chains. He had been quick to suggest they search away from Black Isle, then tried to dismiss it altogether by throwing blame toward crimes long since exposed.

She was quite certain that the horse was not locked in chains over bairns that were sold many years ago. There must be another reason, and she and Riley would uncover it. Shaw knew that horse, she was certain. Every time it came up, he lost his usual carefree demeanor. Perhaps she needed to force him to visit the faerie glen so he could see it for himself.

Black Isle was full of mysteries. Now there were two more for them to solve. Which was more important? The horse or Shaw's blackmailer?

Shaw's opinion was clear—he'd gladly forget all about the horse. But Tara knew she never would.

CHAPTER EIGHT

S HAW SENT HIS horse into a gallop. He wanted to get this over with. Not wanting anyone to know his destination, he'd left Eddirdale Castle before the sun was up, hoping to catch Dougal before he started his morning's tasks, whatever they might be. The trip to Inverness had revealed little except the gossip about the sheriff. But the inquisition coming from Ethan and soon to be Marcas was not going to be as bad as the one from Tara.

Guilt that flowed through him every time she looked at him, as if she questioned his character because of the blackmail. Should he be honest with her?

Not yet. No one would understand. He had to resolve this issue in another way, one that allowed them all to forget the word blackmail.

Dougal MacKinnie had been his closest friend in their younger days. Though Dougal was heir to the lairdship and Shaw was the youngest son, that difference never mattered to the two of them. They'd gone to all the festivals together, challenged each other in their training and in private competitions, then supported each other when they competed at festivals.

They'd both been successful with the sword in tourneys and games. Though Shaw was a bit better than Dougal, he hadn't flaunted it. The friendship had been more important than anything.

Their favorite activity, as they came of age, had been chasing lasses and light skirts, though Shaw's father kept him respectable. His sire made sure he didn't go too far, constantly lecturing him about the fact that if he ever took a lass's maidenhead, he'd be married within a sennight.

That had kept Shaw in line. Dougal had had no such compunctions nor faced any such consequences.

As they grew, the two had been drawn to different kinds of relationships with lasses. While Dougal continued to chase anything in a skirt, Shaw became more deliberate about who he kept company with. He had even thought about marriage occasionally but hadn't found any particular lass he'd been interested in.

Until that fateful summer.

He and Dougal had met Eschina MacHeth and her distant relative from the mainland, Lucretia Baird, who was visiting Black Isle for the summer, at a spring festival and seen them two more times after that. They'd taken the two lasses hunting, chasing across the meadow and into the woods on horseback, but the worst had happened. Nothing had been the same since, though he tried his best to make it totally vanish from his memory. Even now, he refused to allow the memory, shoving it back into the deepest corner of his mind.

Someone must have been watching in those woods, seen exactly what happened.

Shaw could not risk the truth getting out.

He drew closer to MacKinnie land and slowed his horse, doing his best to maintain control, to prevent any memories entering his mind and ruining his purpose today. He had two topics to speak to Dougal about, and neither could wait.

There was only one guard at the gate, whom he didn't know, but the guard knew him. "Why are you here, Matheson? Have you not done enough damage to our clan?"

The battle to free his sister, Gisela, from Donald MacKinnie's schemes to wed her had been no fault of the Mathesons. The healers among them suggested that Donald's erratic behavior and death had been due to illness, though Padraig Grant had hurried that death along a wee bit. Still, it was Donald's own actions—kidnapping Gisela foremost among them—that had done the true harm to the MacKinnie clan.

"'Tis in the past. I need to speak with Dougal. If you do not wish for me to enter, then send him out."

The guard nodded and disappeared. Shaw stayed on his horse, backing off from the gates in case anyone else came out.

He didn't have to wait long before the gates opened. Dougal rode through and headed straight for Shaw. He was handsome, with his strong jaw and light brown hair, and the three parallel scars along one jawline made most describe him as "interesting." Those scars were yet another reminder Shaw didn't want, and thus one of the many reasons he hadn't attempted to preserve their friendship. Dougal pointed back in the direction Shaw had come from. "Away from the coastline. 'Tis fishing time."

Shaw allowed Dougal to choose the spot where they could talk without fear of being overheard. He took him up a hill into the forest, a scenic area he'd never been before. Once they stopped, he turned toward Dougal, surprised to see the red sand cliffs rising from the coastline. From their vantage point, he could see the boats in Beauly Firth, the jackdaws darting about. The faerie glen wasn't far, though it was more inland in the thick trees of the forest. Even this far into the forest, no one would overhear a word they said.

Dougal asked, "What do you want, Matheson?"

"I need to know if you're being squeezed for more coin."

Dougal let out a deep sigh, and a look of defeat crossed his features, telling Shaw all he needed to know. "Aye, the bastard is relentless and greedy."

"Mayhap 'tis time to band together and find a way to stop this." He didn't know what they could do, but anything was worth a try.

"Do you have a proposal?"

"Nay, but you know the sheriff of Cromarty— he was there that day. I've heard that he likes to take more coin than the king is due. Keeps the extra for himself. And he's rumored to be involved in other blackmail schemes as well. Apparently, he was involved in the dispute between Padraig and your brother. Took payment to lock up Padraig."

"Aye, Donald paid him to lock Grant up until he could wed your sister. Didn't work, obviously." Dougal ran his hand through his curly dark hair, looking as frustrated as Shaw felt.

"Think you he could be the one blackmailing us?"

"Nay, he's too brash. If it were him, he wouldn't hide himself. He'd come straight to both of us and demand payment."

Shaw considered this, knowing he'd dismissed the possibility many times before for the same reason. He sighed. "If I were to guess, I'd be thinking it to be someone neither of us knows."

"Aye. And how will we ever find someone we don't know?"

Shaw had no answer for him. "We need to compare notes on meeting places and times. Do you go directly or send someone?"

"I send someone I trust completely."

"Has that person ever seen any evidence of who is doing this?" Shaw asked.

"Nay, and neither have I when I've gone with him."

Shaw cursed. "I've tried following, and I always come up empty. At first it seemed like the person who collects the money doesn't come for days. But then earlier this year I looked inside the box we've been told to use, and it has a chute that goes below the building, so I don't know where it goes. Somewhere under the town stable in Beauly. There must be a cellar, but I've never found the way in."

"Nay, we've never gone to any stable. 'Tis an old log in the forest for us. Occasionally a place along the coastline."

"We're closer to Beauly than you are, so 'tis probably why we go there."

"I'm certain the bastard sends others to do his work. If we ever caught anyone, it would probably be some lad or lass. He's too smart to risk getting caught."

Shaw had discussed the same with Sammy and told him to look out for even the least likely person coming and going. Villains hired others to do their work. "You mean too cowardly to do his own dirty work. He's got no bollocks."

"Seems to me you believe you know who the guilty party is. Share your suspicions with me."

"Nay, I don't know. If I did, I would confront the weak-kneed bastard."

Dougal snorted. "You refer to him as though he's a fool. I think we are the fools. We're the ones still paying."

Shaw couldn't argue that point. "My patience with this is near spent. 'Tis time for me to focus on uncovering who the blackmailer is. I'll get Ethan onto it. He's quite logical and good at puzzles."

Dougal took a long look at him. "If you think you have any idea who it is at all, please let me know. I'll go with you when you confront the bastard. 'Tis my coin too."

Shaw nodded, though he truly had no idea what to do next. He and Sammy had spent half a day at the Beauly stables, trying everything to get into that chute to see where the coin had gone on a couple of occasions. He'd tried to get his hand inside, but had only been able to squeeze his fingers in. Sammy's hand had fit, but he hadn't felt anything but the wooden sides of the chute and a bit of a breeze wafting up from below. That draft was why he thought there must be a cellar of some kind. When asked, the stable owner had just shrugged and offered no insight. Shaw had no desire to explain why he wanted to know about the odd slot on the side of the building. "So do you have any ideas, other than just not making the payments anymore?"

"Shaw, we can't stop and risk anyone finding out what happened. My sire cannot know. He'd disown me and I'd lose the lairdship. Do not think of revealing the truth to anyone."

Shaw nodded, knowing exactly how Dougal felt. "I haven't said anything to anyone but Ethan." He let the matter drop for the moment and turned to the other question on his mind. "Do you know of anyone who has a horse like the one we lost that day?"

Dougal frowned, thinking for a long moment. Then he shook his head. "Nay, I cannot think of one. I know of other white horses, but none with the same markings. Why?"

Shaw knit his brows. "Someone mentioned seeing a horse like it in the faerie glen. Perhaps someone is playing a trick. Some kind of taunt."

"Don't let anything else spook you. Aye, we're being blackmailed for more, but naught else has changed. The only reason it has changed is greed, pure and simple."

"I hope you'll return the favor, if you ever find the bastard, and come and get me so I can exercise my fists on the fool's face," Shaw said, his blood boiling anew at the greed of the villain, his powerlessness to stop him, and the thought that Tara's unicorn vision might be a cruel joke. "He'll pay for all he's put us through."

He'd cost him plenty of coin, but worse, he could cost him the lass he was falling in love with. The look in her eyes had told him so, and he couldn't allow that to happen.

Tara took a seat by the hearth with Riley and Jennet after she finished her evening meal. They'd had several clan members to visit in the village with various ailments, so their day had been busy. She had been hoping to see Shaw in the great hall, since she hadn't seen him in the two days since they returned from Inverness. If she had her way, she'd be hiding in the bushes or dark corners with him sneaking more kisses. But he'd rarely been at the castle; she assumed he was on patrol, but perhaps he'd also been seeking a way to end the blackmail.

The blackmail. That word that made her hesitate. It made her question Shaw's entire character. Why wouldn't he share the full truth of the issue? If he didn't have something to hide, something serious, why would he be paying?

Perhaps the next time she saw him, he would explain in more detail. After all, the time they'd spent in Inverness hadn't been private, but in company with Ethan and Jennet, the guards, and the vendors and residents of the burgh. Ever since she'd found out about it, though, the subject had occupied her mind more than she cared to admit.

They needed to talk.

The outer door opened, and she turned around to see who had arrived, hoping for Shaw's handsome face. Surprise stilled her for a moment. Her mother and father were standing there.

"Mama?"

Riley yelled, "Papa!"

Tara hoped her parents hadn't noticed the two different levels of excitement in their greetings. Riley's had been pure joy, hers a worried question. Why had they come, without warning or invitation?

She knew, deep in her heart, that if they were here, something was wrong. She crossed the room with Riley to greet them.

"Brin is hale?" Tara asked. Her brother came in right then, and she sighed with relief. While she was happy to see her parents, she didn't wish to hear that anyone was hurt or ill. "Mama, I'm so pleased to see you, but has something happened?"

Brigid and Jennet hurried to join them, gushing with joy. Jennet was named after her Aunt Jennie, and they'd always had a special bond. She greeted her with an embrace. "Aunt Jennie, 'tis so nice to see you here."

Brigid jumped into her hostess duties. "Please come in! We just finished the evening meal, but we have much left over."

The whole group made their way back to the hearth. Her mama looked at Brigid's bairns and lifted Tiernay up from the floor where he played. "And who is this wee laddie? This must be Tiernay."

Marcas, Ethan, and Shaw returned just as Brigid finished introducing the children and joined them. Brigid made more introductions, then went into the kitchens to arrange for a light supper for the group, encouraging them to sit at the large table where they could all fit. Cheerful voices filled the hall as they greeted one another, chatter and laughter abounding.

Tara followed Brigid into the kitchens, where she found her speaking with Nonie and Edda, arranging for six bowls of pottage to be brought out along with trays of bread, fruit, and cheese. Marcas and his brothers had missed the evening meal, though Tara had no idea why. Brigid had just shrugged her shoulders, apparently used to having Marcas late because of pressing matters. Once her cousin finished with her instructions and the other two women hustled away, Tara grabbed Brigid's arm.

"What are they doing here? Brigid, something must be wrong."

Brigid gave her a puzzled look, but then shrugged her shoulders. "Mayhap they miss their daughters."

"Nay, you don't understand. Your mother and father travel all over the land and no one questions it. My father hates leaving home. He wouldn't come unless Riley or I were near death. I don't

like that they're here without any warning. And
Brin came along!" Her eyes widened, though she
tried to control her expression.

"Calm down, Tara. Everything will be fine,"
Brigid said. "Allow your parents to eat and rest
before you confront them with your fears. If they
have something to tell you, I'm sure they will
soon."

The door to the kitchens opened, and there
stood her mother. Though she had a smile on her
face, she looked worried.

"Mama, what is it?" This she couldn't ignore.

Her mother shook her head, her lips trembling
in that way she had just before tears streaked her
cheeks. "Naught. I was just…we heard…are you
hale?"

"Of course I'm hale." She rushed over to her
mother and gave her a swift hug. "What did you
hear?"

"All sorts of things about Black Isle. When
Padraig and Gisela came to stay, one of the guards
they were traveling with said they overheard some
men talking about coming after 'the Cameron
lass.' They didn't recognize the men and were
unable to catch them. Padraig assured us you
were well protected, but we just heard another
tale of someone after a Cameron lass. You're both
here now, you and Riley. Your father and I have
been sick with worry. And so much has happened
here recently." Her gaze went from Tara to Brigid
and then back to her daughter.

Tara had no idea who might have plans to harm
her or even spread such a rumor. "They must

have heard wrong. No one has bothered me, and I don't know why they would." She glanced over at Brigid, hoping she had something to add.

"Aunt Jennie, all is well here. We've had some unusual situations, surely, with Jennet being accused of witchery and the events around Gisela's betrothal, but all is well now. The threat is gone. We've heard of no danger or problems."

"Is there some group still upset with Clan Matheson?" Tara's mother asked. "Is MacKinnie out to pay you back for what happened to his son? Something must be stirring here."

"Nay, naught, Auntie. Please don't worry so. We have a good number of guards now. And you know we can count on Uncle Alex if we need him. His men can get here in a day if they ride hard. And you know my sire. He still stops in for a visit here and there. In fact, he hasn't been here of late, so we're expecting to see him soon."

Uncle Logan hadn't been here since Jennet's witchery trial, so Tara had to agree with Brigid on that note, nodding along. "It is about time for him to make an appearance." Tara handed a linen square to her mother. "Mama, mop your tears and come sit by the fire. You're cold. Have you a chill? The bairns are sweet as can be. Perhaps you could tell them a story. They love to listen to tales."

Her mother patted her cheek and said, "That sounds lovely, Tara. I'll go find them. Come with me?"

"Of course," she said. Her mother had only to ask and Tara would willingly grant her anything, but spending time with the bairns was hardly a difficulty.

They left the kitchens and almost ran into Shaw coming out of the great hall. "Oh, Tara, I was coming to see if all was well."

"Aye, Shaw, all is well. We were just returning to the hall." She set her hand in the crook of his elbow to give her mother the idea that Shaw meant more to her than Ethan or Marcas. Her mother's gaze fell to her hand on Shaw's arm, but she dropped it when he wrapped his arm around Tara's shoulders. A little smile floated across her mother's mouth, and her eyebrows went up.

Shaw cleared his throat. "I would have preferred to ask your husband first, but since you are here, I'll ask you. May I have your permission to court your daughter? I've become quite fond of her." A blush darkened his cheeks.

Tara's heart nearly burst at watching Shaw turn from big hulking warrior to nervous lad in front of her mother, but she kept her thoughts to herself, stifling her urge to giggle.

"Ah, well, you should probably speak with her father, but I am agreeable. The Matheson brothers are known for their honor, skill, and strength."

"He's a fine man, Mama," Tara said.

Brigid, grinning broadly, nodded next to her. "Agreed. They are all fine men, Aunt Jennie."

"I'm sure they are, my dear Brigid. I may have a drink with my supper. Have you any wine?" Her mother's brown hair was plaited, but many strands had loosened over the travel. Her skin was luminous, something Tara wished to mimic, but couldn't seem to master. She was more like her father than her mother. The fact that her mother asked for wine told her the trip had been especially grueling for the dear woman. Most likely from worry, rather than exertion.

Who would have anything against her?

"Aye, being so close to Inverness we are blessed with a fine selection. I'll bring a bottle from France for you." Brigid disappeared to the wine cellar.

Tara said to her mother, "I hope that now that you've seen I'm well, Mama, you will cease your worries."

Her mother cupped her cheeks and said, "'Tis wonderful to see your smiling face again, daughter. Shaw, I expect you to protect my lass."

"With my life," he said, his chest puffing out a wee bit.

Her mother headed back into the hall, and they followed her over to the hearth, where the children played. It wasn't long before her father made his way over to them.

Shaw greeted him with a small bow of respect. "I would like your permission to court your daughter, sir. She is as fine a lass as ever I have met."

Her mother looked up at her father, a smile on her face. Kara tugged her back to help with a very important task. "My lady, would you help me dress my doll?"

"Of course. I would love to, but I am not your lady. I'm your great-aunt now, because your papa married Brigid, and you must call me Aunt Jennie."

Kara looked to Brigid who nodded her encouragement.

Aedan Cameron looked at Tara, taking in his daughter's countenance. "Before I answer this young man, I have questions for you, daughter. You are hale? I'm sure your mother told you why we're here. Those blasted tales keep arising, and we cannot dismiss them as mere rumor."

"Aye, she did. Naught has happened. I am enjoying my time here...and Shaw's company."

"Are you now? How long ago did this interest start?" She caught the playful tease in his voice, the sparkle in his blue eyes. He glanced over at Shaw, but then back to her.

"Not long, Papa. We've just become closer, 'tis all." She thought of their time in Inverness, thinking how fortunate they were that her parents hadn't come while they were gone or that they hadn't stopped at the inn where they'd stayed and heard tales of just how close they'd gotten.

"Shaw, you are a true Highlander? You will protect my daughter with your life?"

"Of course, my lord."

Aedan nodded and said, "You have my permission for now. I look forward to getting to know you better. We are worried about our daughter's safety, so I expect you will help watch over her."

Her first thought was she could use their trip as evidence that she was indeed safe, but second thought made her rethink the wisdom of the explanation. Her parents would see for themselves that all was well.

Shaw thanked him and stepped over to speak with Marcas for a moment. Her father waited until he was gone, then said, "We'll be here for a short time, thanks to Marcas's hospitality, so we'd be pleased to get to know him better before we leave."

"How long are you staying?" She had no idea what their plan was and hoped they weren't upset at her question.

His eyes bored into hers. "Until we convince our two daughters 'tis time to come home."

Tara's knees nearly buckled.

CHAPTER NINE

THE FOLLOWING MORN, Shaw and Tara took off across the meadow, giving their horses the chance to gallop as much as they wished in the fleeting midday sun. He could just hear her laughter, swept back by the wind along with her hair, as she tried to keep up with him. He'd had no better idea about the rumors that had brought her parents to Black Isle than she did, when she asked him about it that morning. But he hadn't kissed her in forever, so he'd talked her into going for a ride—not a difficult task, he was happy to discover. She'd convinced him to ride to the faerie glen. Making sure to handle everything properly with her parents around, he brought a few guards with them, and they rode in a loose curve behind and alongside Tara and him.

Once they slowed their horses, Tara said in a low voice, "Have you not an errand to send the guards on, Shaw?"

Shaw grinned, hoping he was interpreting her meaning correctly. "Do I sense someone yearning for more kisses, lass?"

"That you do, my lord. Will you accommodate

me?" She batted her eyelashes at him, making her interest clear.

He didn't even try to hide his grin, instead moving his horse close enough to hers for him to lean over and kiss her cheek, which sent her into a flurry of giggles.

Hell, but he liked this woman, more than any other. If it weren't for all the haunted reminders from seeing Dougal and the blackmail hanging over his head—and depleting his funds—he might ask her to marry him. Tara was exactly the type of lass he longed to have at his side. Ever since they met, he'd been drawn to her. Whenever they spent time together at a festival, they passed the day in laughter and delight. He loved kissing her even more, and there simply was no one more beautiful than Tara Cameron. But most of all, he loved to talk with her. She knew so much more than he did, was such a good listener, and always had good advice for him. For some odd reason, she made him feel invincible, yet he had no idea why.

Then why didn't he dare trust her with the truth? Because the truth was too painful. If he were ever fortunate enough to get rid of his blackmailer, he'd be forever grateful. But he couldn't help but wonder how her parents saw him and what they would think if they knew of the blackmail. Was he good enough to marry the daughter of a laird?

Had he been more foolish than most youth? Questions haunted him every day, and yet he had no answer. Much as he tried to convince himself he was trustworthy and honorable, every part of his being screamed to be careful because he didn't deserve her. If the truth came out, she'd never marry him, and even if she agreed, her parents would never give their permission.

For now, he did his best to pretend that day had never happened. Reason told him that if he and Dougal could find the blackmailer, put an end to their torment, he could marry Tara with a clear conscience. Live an unfettered life of happiness.

Live a life without this constant fear of the truth being discovered, something always hanging over him. This need to always look over his shoulder could end.

They crossed the ridge before the faerie glen and found a place to tie their horses. Shaw signaled one of the guards. "Patrol the area. We'll only be a few moments." He helped her down and gave her waist a quick squeeze.

She wasn't as trim and thin as many other lasses, and he was glad. Her curves were glorious, and he longed to explore her softness. His father had always told the three lads they had to choose a lass with wide hips in order to give them many bairns.

He took Tara's hand and led her closer to the falls. "Do you know that there is another waterfall behind this one? Most people stop here and go no farther. They're equally beautiful."

"Truly? Will you show me? Riley and I didn't go any further—the horse came to us here."

He turned her toward him and cupped her face. Bending his mouth to hers, he kissed her thoroughly. He'd been imagining this moment for days. Her lips were softer, more welcoming than he remembered. He was even more pleased when she moved closer, melding her body against his. He angled his head, and she parted her lips with a sigh. He swept his tongue inside to mate with hers, humming at her sweetness. She matched his every move, returning his licks and nips and asking for more, though she spoke not.

Hell, but they would be fabulous together. He knew it.

He ended the kiss, then returned for a final quick taste, smiling at how swollen and rosy her lips appeared. The kiss had reached his toes, and her glazed eyes told him she felt the same.

"Come," he said. "I'll show you the other falls. 'Tis a bit of a trek, but I think you'll like it."

He led her along a worn path to the left of the first waterfall, up a hill and behind it until the sound of the second waterfall became louder than the first one.

Shaw froze. Standing knee-deep in the middle of the pool at the base of the cascade stood a white horse, facing away from them. It looked so much like his old horse Zinna, he had to stop himself from calling out her name.

"Look, it's Riley's horse," Tara said softly, a little breathless. "I hope it will come over to us."

Shaw's head nearly exploded, but he controlled himself. It was a white horse, without a doubt, but he wasn't close enough to see the markings on its ear. Then it turned around, the horn sprouting from between its eyes, growing long and looking as though it would touch the tree branches. The horse looked like his old mount, but clearly it couldn't be, since it was indeed a unicorn. He prayed it didn't have the same markings. It couldn't be, could it? The hair on his arms stood on end as he took in everything about the beast in front of them, desperately searching for differences.

He'd never forget that day. The horse had belonged to him, but he'd allowed Lucretia to ride her. The mare had been one of his favorites, so seeing her dead that day had been one of the worst moments of his life. But a horse with two broken legs could not be saved, and he knew it. It had been a mercy to end the injured animal's suffering.

Fortunately, Dougal had done the task for him.

The horse drank from the pool, then lifted its head and stared directly at him.

"Look, Shaw. 'Tis a true unicorn. It doesn't have the gold chains today."

Tara moved to step closer, and he grabbed her hand. "Please don't, Tara." Just the fact that the horse looked so much like his lost mare gave him an eerie feeling. Why was it here? "You need to be careful. Neither one of us know that animal." This area was a faerie glen, after all. Faeries were capricious creatures and more likely to play tricks than be kind, and everyone on Black Isle had heard of odd occurrences happening here. But never a dead horse coming back to life.

Or becoming a unicorn, the horse of legend.

"Don't worry. I'll not go into the water. Just

closer to the edge so she can come to me."

"Mayhap she won't. You don't know for sure 'tis the same horse as before, do you?"

"Aye, I'm quite sure it is. She looks the same to me. 'Tis Riley's horse that we saw before. It spoke to Riley. I wonder if we'll be able to hear it. I'll know if 'tis the same when I get close enough to see its markings."

Tara held her hand out to the horse, but Shaw couldn't move, his gaze locked on the animal.

His horse.

His dead horse.

His dead horse transformed into a unicorn.

It moved toward them then circled Tara and came straight to him, stepping out of the pool and onto the bank. The horse neighed cheerfully, stopping a hand's breadth away and pushing its nose toward him in familiar affection. He couldn't stop himself from reaching up and placing his fingers in front of the horse's muzzle, letting her smell him.

And it was as if he leaped back in time to when she was living. "What is that thing between your eyes?" he asked softly.

The horse stepped forward and leaned down, placing its neck on his shoulder. How he wished it hadn't. It gave him a perfect view of the animal's ear. And the marking there he'd never seen on another animal. The beast was showing it to him.

He moved back, his hand coming up to stroke her neck, and he whispered, "I know."

Then he leaned his head against the animal to hide his tears, turning his face away from Tara so she wouldn't see.

This was his horse. His dead horse.

What the hell was happening?

Tara moved to Shaw's side. "You know her, don't you?"

He tipped his head up toward the sky to rid himself of the tears fighting to fall from his eyes. Fortunately, he hadn't completely lost control when he saw the horse up close, heard the familiar neigh she would greet him with.

"Nay, but she's a bonnie one. She reminds me of an old horse I had, but the markings are different. Still makes me sentimental. She's a beauty, aye?"

Hellfire, he'd just lied to the woman he hoped to marry, if he could ever set things to right.

Would it be possible? Or had that one fateful day ruined his life forever?

Tara stood next to him, wondering if he'd just told her the truth about this horse. "What was your horse's name?"

"Zinna. Bonnie Zinna."

The horse whinnied as if she recognized the name.

"What happened to her?"

"An accident. Someone else was riding her, and she took a fall, had to be put down."

"Oh, Shaw," she said, placing her hand on his arm. "I'm so sorry."

Changing the subject, he asked, "What are your parents' plans? Are they still worried you're in danger?"

She grumbled a bit then said, "Papa says he's taking us both home. They'll stay a few days and then we'll all go back."

Shaw stood back and took both her hands in his. The horse turned away and disappeared soundlessly into the forest. "Is that what you want?"

"Nay. I haven't told them yet, but I'm not going. I thought to save that argument for another day. I like it here. I'm needed as a healer, and my two cousins have become my best friends. And then there's…"

He tipped her chin up and placed a light kiss on her lips. "There's what?"

"Us? You asked to court me, and I'm enjoying my time with you. I'm not ready for that to end. If we leave, who knows when I might see you again."

"Do you want me to court you? I guess I never asked for your feelings."

She gazed up at him, locking her eyes on his. She liked everything about this man, and she wanted more. But how much did she dare admit? "I'd like to get to know you better. There has been so much chaos since I arrived—the curse, the witch trial, and Donald's madness. I'd just like to have some time together in peace."

He kissed her again, a tender kiss that was soft and warm and delicious. Which did she prefer, the hard, passionate kiss or this soft, tender one?

She liked them both. And she realized she had much she could learn with Shaw.

When he ended the kiss, a voice called out to

them, one of his guards. "Shaw! Ethan's looking for you. Where the hell are you?"

"We'll be right there," he shouted back. He took her hand in his and led her back down the small trail. "Will you attend the MacHeth festival with me on the morrow? I hope your parents won't take you away just yet. Ethan and I are competing in the games in the morn, but after that, I would love to take you around the rest of the festival. Get a bite to eat, buy you a trinket to remember me by, if you do have to go."

"I would love that."

He gave her the widest smile she'd ever seen and waggled his brows at her just before they broke through into the clearing around the lower falls. "I look forward to it."

Tara's heart did a flip unlike anything she'd ever felt before. "I'll have to spend some time with my parents, I'm sure."

"Come with them to the games, then we'll sneak away after I'm finished."

"I'd like that."

Nay, she'd love that, and she'd be counting down the hours.

Shaw had to admit that Tara pleased him more than she would ever know. He lifted her onto her horse, then yelled to Torcall, "Tell Ethan we're on our way. Leave the other guards with us."

Torcall nodded and headed off, motioning for the three other guards to stay with Shaw and Tara.

The ride home passed more quickly than Shaw

liked, and soon they were out of the dense forest. A large rock on their left—taller than a man and wider than three abreast—marked the halfway point. Just as they passed it, Shaw heard a shout. Four riders burst out from behind the boulder. Two men came directly at Tara while the others engaged the guards.

"Grab the lass!"

Before he could reach Tara, her horse reacted to the attack by bolting forward, toward their attackers, giving one the chance to lift her off her horse and haul her onto his. He headed directly into the trees.

"Tara!" Shaw locked his eyes on his quarry, urging his horse after him in chase. Fortunately he rode one of his fastest stallions, one who loved a race and rarely lost. They followed the man with Tara through the trees, crashing through brush, ducking to keep from taking a stick to the eye. "I'm right behind you. Fight him, Tara."

They raced uphill, into the steeper territory of the isle. But there was no way in hell Shaw would lose Tara. She was his hope. His future. They leaped a fallen log, slid down a steep slope, then the forest flattened and opened up. His stallion put on a burst of speed, and they caught up with the other man, racing neck and neck through a clearing. Shaw drew his dagger and jabbed, embedding the blade in the bastard's side. The man jerked and cursed, but didn't fall.

Noticing that they were headed back to dense forest, he knew this was his best chance. He shouted to Tara, "Grab the reins if you can!"

Then he launched himself at the fool, knocking him off his horse. They rolled together across the ground, but Shaw came out on top and pinned the other man, pummeling his face until he stopped struggling. He grabbed him by the throat and yelled, "Why?"

The man only gurgled, then turned his head aside and spat blood and at least one tooth.

He had to know why. "Who hired you? Who were you after? Why the lady?" He'd heard enough from Aedan Cameron to know that this was no fluke or reiver. This was a paid man, and he needed answers.

Hoofbeats made him look up. Tara had turned the horse and was returning to him. She jumped to the ground and went after Shaw's stallion, still prancing not far away.

"Talk!" he shouted at the would-be kidnapper.

When he didn't speak, Shaw tightened his grip on his airway, choking the breath out of him. He'd never been so angry. Never. Seeing Tara in that man's hands was more than he could handle.

Now he understood Brigid's favorite comment about her father. She'd always teased people that if they touched her without her permission, her sire would kill them.

"Who sent you?"

"He paid me coin…" The man gasped out, so Shaw let up. He needed the information more than the satisfaction of killing him.

"Go ahead and I might let you live. Who and why?"

"Wants the Cameron lass. I just did what he said for two gold coins."

"Who?"

"The sheriff. I don't know which one. Some sheriff wants the lass who can get him all the coin. 'Tis all I know." The man spit another stream of blood off to the side, the fear in his gaze giving Shaw a small sense of satisfaction.

Ethan came behind him. "Let him up, and I'll take care of him, Shaw. You've done enough."

Shaw glanced over his shoulder at his brother. If not for him, he would beat the man to death, probably. He could easily ignore the cuts and bruises already paining him on his fists. "He's all yours, Ethan. Take him to *our* sheriff."

Shaw released the man and stood, looking around for Tara. He rushed over to her, though she met him partway and launched herself at him. He expected tears, but he didn't get them. "Many thanks to you, Shaw."

He tugged her close and cupped her face. "Did he hurt you? If he did, I owe him a few more bruises." He had never been so upset over anything. He shook with the remnants of his anger and relief. "He touched you, and I didn't like it."

"Nay, I'm fine. He was too busy trying to escape you." She grinned. "You sound just like my uncle Logan." Then she leaned toward him and whispered. "And I like it."

Then she did the last thing he would have expected. She lifted his fist and kissed each knuckle that was bruised or cut.

"Ah, lass. He did make me daft. Means I'm daft for you."

CHAPTER TEN

SHAW STOOD AT the edge of the field where the morning's competitions would take place, warming his muscles up for his event. There would be swordplay, archery, and the heavy events—log tossing, hammer throws, and the like. He had signed up for the sword tourney. He'd learned much from the Grants and the Ramsays over the last months. He especially valued Connor Grant's lessons, and though he wasn't as muscular as the other man, he had learned many of his tricks.

He rubbed his sore knuckles, glad he wasn't going to participate in anything that would pain him more. Ethan had told him he'd never seen anyone so crazed. He had to admit he'd never felt it before either.

But the hardest part had been admitting to her parents why the man had stolen her away, though he didn't understand why anyone would think Tara had access to any unusual amount of coin. Her father had wrapped his arm around his daughter, kissed the top of her head, and thanked Shaw for bringing her back.

He had to let that go for now and focus on the

events. There were enough people around that he wasn't expecting trouble this day. Tara would be attending with her parents and Riley, along with Brigid and Jennet, if he were to guess.

And probably a score of Cameron guards surrounding her. No one would touch her this day.

He and his brothers wore their plaids proudly, grateful simply to be there for the festival this time. The last MacHeth festival had taken place during the curse, when his clanmates had been dying in droves.

Clan Matheson was back. And they would prove their prowess this day. Ethan was competing in archery, and other Matheson clan members would be throwing hammers and logs, and piping and dancing across on the other side of the festival grounds. Marcas had decided not to compete and would be spending the day with his bairns and new wife.

The marshal of the games declared the beginning of the swordsmanship competition and announced the pairings of the competitors. Shaw would be going against a MacKinnie guard for his first round, but not one he knew well. He nodded in satisfaction. He preferred his opponents to be strangers.

Each pair was to fight until one of them lost his weapon or first blood was drawn, when the judge for each fight would call a halt and declare the winner. At the end of the first round, the winners would then be matched against each other. There were four rounds total.

He needed to make it to the final round.

He scanned the area, pleased to see Tara had just arrived arm in arm with her sister, their parents strolling along behind them. Guards walked in a semicircle around them. Not a score but enough to protect her. She smiled and waved, so he approached them and gave a small bow.

"Greetings, all."

"We came to wish you well in your fights, Shaw," Aedan Cameron said. "Tara tells me you've had good training from the Grant and Ramsay warriors."

"Aye, I learned much from Gavin Ramsay, but even more from Connor Grant when he was here."

"You won't find a better swordsman than Connor Grant. Mayhap his brother or his sire, but Connor is powerful. I wish you luck."

"My thanks to you, my lord. I hope to walk with your daughter afterward, if I may."

"If Tara is agreeable, then you have my permission." Aedan locked eyes with him, and Shaw nodded solemnly, understanding the trust Aedan was putting in him. Then he heard his name called to the field and bade the Camerons farewell.

He moved to his assigned place and removed his tunic in preparation. Marcas came up behind him and clasped his shoulders. "You'll win the first three rounds easily, Shaw. You've worked hard and it shows. You're stronger and taller than your opponent this round, which gives you a great advantage."

"My greatest difficulty is going to be focusing on the competition and not on what took place yesterday."

Marcas moved to face him. "Aedan Cameron will not take her away forever. He may take her for a bit, but you will learn where Cameron land is and the best way to make the journey. What happened yesterday explains nearly all the things he's heard in the last weeks. The sheriff is intent on stealing some easy coin. Perhaps he's heard that Tara has access to Lochluin Abbey's wealth. I should have suspected someone would try something when word got out and been more alert. But with everything else that has taken place, I missed it."

"Aye. The abbey is close to Cameron Castle, Tara tells me. I must put it out of my head for now, though. It will feel good to focus on the swing of my sword against my opponent. I worry if I lose, Cameron will think me not good enough for his daughter." A little lie, but a harmless one. His past was more likely to cause Cameron's disapproval than his performance in a festival list.

"You saved his daughter yesterday, and she's the first to thank you. Any father wants someone who would give their life for their daughter, and you've proven yourself on that already. Stop thinking on it and focus on the contest. We have time to worry about the other issue."

"Many thanks, Marcas. You are correct." He glanced over his shoulder at the MacKinnie he would face and caught him staring at him, an expression of disgust on his face.

"Don't allow the bastard to bother you with his odd looks. He'll not stand a chance. Wish Connor was here to watch you." Marcas slapped his shoulder and stepped back, moving close to Brigid and picking Tiernay up. "We'll watch Uncle Shaw win, my lad."

"Hurrah for Uncah Shaw!" Kara called out, making him smile. How he adored his niece and nephew, and he gave them both a quick wink.

Tara and her family were standing not far away. He wanted to impress her, but he could not allow himself to be distracted. Connor had told him over and over again, "Shut everything out of your mind except your opponent. Especially lasses."

He'd never had a problem with that before, but after tasting Tara's sweet lips he now had to work to heed Connor's warning.

He was called to the center, so he stepped forward, swinging his sword in a quick figure eight to adjust his grip…and maybe show off just a little. He couldn't help but notice how his opponent's sword seemed to shrink compared to his. He had to thank Connor again, this time for going with him to the armorer in Beauly where he guided him on how to get the strongest sword. It had taken Shaw a few days to gain the strength to lift it, but now he was grateful.

Had he not trained with this sword, he'd never have been able to take down the bastard who'd tried to capture Tara. The weapon was the length of a pony, with a fine double-edged blade. It cut through his practice dummies smooth as butter. As he swung it now, he relished the weight of it.

When the judge for his bout raised his hand, he and the MacKinnie man stepped forward.

Shaw waited, poised in his fighter's stance, until the judge's hand dropped. Then he went straight at his opponent, the clash of steel blades ringing out, drawing a roar of excitement from the crowd.

"You'll die, scum," the warrior said to him.

Shaw contained his surprise. He had participated in a few contests before, but he didn't recall ever speaking to his opponent. He ignored him, using a move Connor had taught him, hitting the man hard from the side, knocking him to his knees. The crowd roared their approval, urging Shaw to draw blood, but he stepped back, allowing the other man to get back on his feet. He wanted a fair fight, no question in anyone's mind about who was the stronger swordsman.

The man came forward, swung at him, and whispered, "You're in trouble, Matheson. All of you."

Shaw didn't react, Gavin's teachings echoing in his mind, his warning about how weaker fighters will use any tactic to unsettle you, anything for the win. *Focus.*

He did. He roared, swinging his sword in a powerful side arc, catching the guardsman's sword with the flat of his blade, a move that sent it cartwheeling across the field. The closest spectators drew back from the spinning weapon in alarm. Then they burst into raucous cheers.

"Winner!" The judge raised the small flag he held over Shaw's head.

His opponent nodded to him, looking like a

good sport to those watching, but Shaw caught the man's whisper under the cheers of the crowd: "You'll pay."

Marcas and Ethan both came up to congratulate him, pounding him on the back. Naturally Ethan had noticed the MacKinnie man's tricks.

"What did he say to you, Shaw? I saw him speak. He was trying to rattle you, was he not?"

Shaw looked over at Tara, a wide smile on her face as she applauded. He returned her grin and gave her a small bow, but then turned to his brothers, repeating what the warrior had said. "What the hell does it mean, Marcas?"

Marcas shook his head. "I don't know, but I've learned not to ignore rumors like the one Aedan Cameron brought us. It could all be related. There were three other men with the one who attacked you yesterday, but they got away. Mayhap he is one of them. We need to find out if he was just trying to rattle you, or if he was making a specific threat. He's a MacKinnie, and they're still angry with us over Donald and Gisela. This event is a perfect place for us to try to find out more." Marcas sighed. "I'd hoped we'd seen the end of trouble for our family."

"I'll find out what I can at the archery contest," Ethan said. "We should all keep our ears alert to rumors."

An uneasy feeling crawled up Shaw's neck, and it had to do with Riley, Tara, and a white horse. Someone called his name, so he turned to look behind him, away from most of the crowd, including Tara.

Eschina MacHeth stood there, motioning for him to come over. He hadn't seen her in years, not since the accident with the horse. He walked toward her, hoping Tara wasn't watching.

"Greetings, Eschina, how do you fare?"

"I am well. 'Twas a fine display of prowess, Shaw. I don't recall you having such a muscular build."

Eschina had been Dougal's sweetheart for a while, but their courtship had ended the day of the accident. "I haven't seen you in a long while, Eschina. What do you want?" He had no desire to rekindle their acquaintance. He'd never much liked her, and seeing her only stirred those memories he wished to avoid.

"We must talk. Meet me later tonight at dusk. In the clearing behind the stable." She set a hand on her hip and tipped it in a provocative way. Eschina was beautiful, no doubt, with long blonde hair and a generous bosom she liked to emphasize. Men fawned over her, but Shaw had never been interested. It hadn't taken him long to see her true nature: selfish and vain.

"I have no reason to speak with you, Eschina. If you have something to say to me, say it now."

"You better show up. Or else."

He couldn't help but snort. The world had turned daft around him. Eschina threatened him and his dead horse had come back for a visit.

What else could possibly happen?

Tara's parents went to browse the vendors' stalls once Shaw won his competition, sweeping through one opponent after the other with seeming ease. Greatly relieved to have them gone, she would not have to worry any longer about them catching her drooling over Shaw's physique. At one point, she'd turned away from her parents because her eyes would betray her if they saw her expression.

And once she'd noticed her tongue was hanging out of her mouth.

The man was fabulous, his long hair tied back with a leather tie. His skin carried a fine sheen of sweat from his exertion, nothing like the dripping sweat of the men he faced—if they even lasted long enough against him to get tired.

No, Shaw swung his sword as though it were an extension of him, moving it easily in different paths that kept his opponent guessing. And kept her happily admiring the ripple of his muscles across his back, in his arms, even in his calves.

She caught herself wondering at one point if his arse muscles would ripple the way his back did. She'd giggled, and her mother gave her an odd look. Chastising herself because she feared Shaw may have heard as well, she'd stopped her daydreaming and watched the fierce Highlander in front of her.

Her Highlander. The one who'd protected her by chasing after a man who'd tried to steal her away for coin. If she wasn't careful, she'd fall in love with him.

Hard.

The moment the judge declared Shaw the champion and the competition over, Tara strode onto the field, eager to congratulate him, but he walked in the opposite direction, summoned by someone's call. She stopped halfway across the list and watched.

That lass again. That thin, curvaceous lass he'd spoken with before, the gorgeous one with the long straight hair that she wore unplaited. Who was she?

Riley came up next to her. "She means naught to him," her sister said as if Tara had spoken her last thought.

"How do you know?"

"His body says he doesn't wish to speak with her. He feels forced."

"I wonder who she is. She surely is beautiful," Tara whispered, hoping no one but her dear sister would hear her. Jealousy dripped from her words, and she knew it.

"She has evil eyes."

"Evil eyes? How can you tell from so far away?"

Riley shrugged. "I just know she has an evil core. Only interested in herself. I'll be interested to learn who she is."

"Do you think he'll be honest?"

"Aye, Shaw may not reveal all, but I believe he'll be truthful."

Shaw turned from the other woman and donned his tunic before heading their way, his medal for winning the swordplay competition around his neck.

"Shite," Tara muttered, without thinking.

Riley tittered. "He did look fine with his shirt off. Did you notice?"

Fine wasn't exactly the word Tara would have used. "Of course I did," she sighed, glancing over at the man with such wistfulness that she wished she was in his arms at that very moment. "I even like his beard." She didn't even care if he was sweaty. Her memory instantly conjured up that sweet view of his muscles rippling with power. It had done something to her core she'd never experienced before.

She'd overheated *down there*. And when she noticed the tingling, she had glanced over at her mother, hoping she hadn't noticed any change in her, but her mother had a small smile on her face and quickly turned away.

"Mama was young once too," Riley said.

"Stop reading my thoughts. 'Tis rude and you know it. I did not give you permission to read my mind."

"I wasn't, but now I know I was right. It was watching your face, the wee bit of saliva coming out of the corner of your mouth telling me all I needed to know." Her sister's grin told *her* all she needed to know.

She gave her sister a playful swat just before Shaw circled the cluster of people around the man he'd just defeated and headed straight for her.

"Congratulations," she called out, waiting until he stood close enough before she stepped in front of him, stood on her tiptoes, and placed a surreptitious kiss on his lips.

He waggled his brows at her with a grin. "Many thanks. I was hoping for a reward from you, but

I feared your parents would make you shy away."

"They may have if my father were standing here, but they went in search of some food. The guards are not far, I'm certain."

Marcas, Brigid, Ethan, and Jennet joined them with the two wee ones, congratulating him on his prowess.

"You were on a level all your own, brother. Your hard work has paid off," Marcas said. "And Ethan won the archery contest too."

Ethan, direct as always, asked, "What did Eschina want?"

Shaw blushed, cast a glance at Tara before answering, "She was more annoying than anything. She had a few comments about how I've built up, but other than that, she had nothing worthwhile to say."

Marcas said, "Good. Her heart is black."

"I know it more than anyone," Shaw said. He took Tara's hand in his and said, "I haven't talked with her in years, so I have no idea why she approached me today. She was Dougal MacKinnie's sweetheart at one time. Never did like her."

"Then cease talking with her," Ethan said.

Tara had to bite her smile back. Ethan always had the simplest view of everything, and he wasn't afraid to share it. She loved his outlook but was secretly glad he wasn't her brother. Dealing with Riley's seer talents was difficult enough. At least Riley knew to keep her thoughts between the two of them. Ethan had few boundaries, though she knew Jennet was working at teaching him to hold his tongue sometimes.

"You are absolutely correct, Ethan, and I will do that. If you don't mind, I'd like to show Tara the rest of the festival. Anyone care to join us?"

Ethan started to speak, but Jennet took his hand and said, "We'll go with Marcas and Brigid. They wished to take the wee ones over to see the ducks by the pond. Riley, will you join us?"

Riley smiled and quickly said, "Aye, I would like that. We'll catch up with you later, sister."

They went their separate ways, and after the others departed Shaw said, "Will your parents be upset if you aren't being escorted by another of your family?"

"Nay, we are here in the open. What could we do?" She glanced up at him innocently, and he grinned at her, his brows telling her he had something less innocent in mind. "I'm sure my sire will have his guards keeping watch on us."

"Shall we sneak away?"

"Nay, not yet. I think we should be seen for a wee bit. I'd not like to get caught sneaking away, or my father will drag me home before you could blink." They reached the edge of the competition field, and Shaw turned them toward the vendors and smaller festival games.

He raised her hand, still held in his, and whispered, "Will they allow this much?"

"I'll allow it. In fact, I prefer it." She laughed and leaned toward him.

"Careful, I'm all sweaty."

"I do not care."

He gazed down at her and asked, "Did I hear

you giggle when I was fighting? I made myself ignore it, but now I must ask."

She rolled her eyes innocently but confessed. "Aye, but I refuse to tell you what I was thinking."

He gave her a puzzled look but didn't say anything.

"All right. I was watching your muscles move when you swung your sword, and that's all I'll say." She couldn't stop the blush from crossing her face.

He laughed and wrapped his arm around her, tugged her close, and kissed her on the lips, sneaking his tongue between her parted lips long enough to mate with hers. She couldn't stop her sigh.

When he ended the kiss, he smiled at her and said, "I'm glad I asked. I'm flattered, and I like that you watch my muscles." He waggled his brow again, neither one of them paying any attention to their surroundings. "Sorry I had to don my tunic again."

When they looked ahead, they nearly walked into her father, standing in front of them with his arms crossed.

"My lord, forgive me. I did not see you there." A quick blush crept up his cheeks.

Tara tried to ease the situation. "Greetings, Papa. You're not checking on us in the middle of the festival, are you? I'm sure if I turn around, I'll see one of your guards behind me."

Her father smiled, clasped Shaw's shoulder and said, "I hear you nearly killed the man yesterday for daring to touch my daughter. I'll keep that in mind. Carry on. Truth is I'm enjoying listening to your happiness, Tara. I've not heard you laugh this much in a long time." He turned to walk away, but then stopped. "Besides, I'm sure my guards are being thoroughly entertained. Your mother told me to leave you alone, so I shall. For now."

He left, striding ahead to catch up to her mother, who was standing there shaking her head.

Shaw said, "I like your father. Is that wrong?"

"Nay. I'm quite fond of him too." To her surprise, a deep voice came from behind him. A man she didn't know came abreast of Shaw and slapped him on the back. "Fine job in the contest, Matheson. Congratulations. The man we sent didn't have any skills."

"My thanks. Tara, this is my old friend Dougal MacKinnie."

Tara smiled and nodded.

"A pleasure to meet such a lovely lass," Dougal said with a smile. "Shaw, if you are still up and about, meet me on the bay at midnight this eve? I have something I'd like to discuss."

"All right."

"Excellent. Until then. My pleasure, Tara Cameron."

After he left, Tara asked, "Have you spoken of me to him before? He knows I'm a Cameron, though you didn't give him my clan name."

Shaw glanced after him. "Nay. Perhaps he's heard of you from some other. We've made no secret of your being with us." But when he returned his attention to her, he looked troubled for a fleeting moment. Then he smiled. "I'll not allow him to distract me from what I wish most of all—to spend time with you. I'm sure you must be hungry. What would you like to eat? Meat pie? Pastry? Pigeon?"

"Hmmm…I think a fruit pastry. Mayhap apple or pear?"

"Your wish I will fulfill if I'm able." They made their way through the vendor stalls, now starting to get crowded as more competitions ended. It would be dusk in another two hours, and families who'd come from farther away would be heading home. He found a pastry vendor and added his voice to the others asking about what was available and calling out their preferences. He was taller than most of the others there and drew the eye of the woman running the stall.

"First choice goes to the one with the medal!" she called out, pointing at Shaw.

He beamed. "My thanks. A pear tart for my lady and a meat pie for myself, whatever kind you have left, please."

The vendor handed out their order in exchange for Shaw's coin.

"It looks luscious," Tara said, accepting her tart.

They made their way away from the crowd to the bank of the pond and stopped in a nice spot under a tree to enjoy their food in peace. The grass was dry and soft, and they sat together, just close enough that Tara could feel his warmth.

"Thank you for coming to watch my bouts. I'm glad you're here—not just at the festival, but part of my home."

"I'm glad too. I like it here."

"And when your parents leave? Your father is not a man to defy."

"Nay, I'll not go."

"I should convince you to stay, but after the events of yesterday, I have to wonder if that's not the right choice. Are others plotting against you? We have no idea which sheriff set those men on you or if he will try again. Mayhap going home will end it, but it could also bring it to the forefront."

"I hadn't thought of that. You think they would follow me back to Cameron land?"

"I think 'tis quite possible. They'll not get near you, especially if I escort you home."

She gazed up at him in shock. "You would do that for me?"

"Aye, of course, if you'll have me," he said. "I'd love to see your home, your castle."

She took another bite of the pastry, and pear juice squirted out of the side, finding its way down her chin. She did her best to catch it, but he reached over with his finger and dabbed it away, then licked his finger clean.

"I want to kiss it away, but I don't dare. I fear I might not be able to stop."

They ate in silence, Tara longing for another touch of his finger, of his lips. She wondered how many other girls he might have touched the same way. "Were you ever with anyone before my cousins and I came to Black Isle? Had you no interest in anyone to marry?"

"In my younger days, there was a lass I liked, but it wasn't to be. And none I've liked so well as you, Tara Cameron." He swallowed the last bite of his pie and caught her gaze. "I think we could be a match. Your parents gave their permission to court you—do you think, after an acceptable amount of time spent courting, you might accept my suit? Would you consider a betrothal? Seeing how happy my brothers have become over the past few months has made me realize that I want the same. But I don't know if I'm worthy of a nobleman's daughter. Did your sire ever think you would marry another?"

"You are worthy, and there is no one else. My parents do not see things that way. My mother's clan believes in choosing your spouse, not in forcing marriages. So if I'm interested, she would agree."

"And are ye interested in a betrothal? 'Tis a big step."

"Aye, Shaw Matheson. I'm interested."

"I'm verra glad to hear it." He helped her to her feet, looking up at the sun. "'Tis an hour's ride home. I suppose we should head back."

They headed toward the area where the Matheson horses waited. Before they reached the rest of their party, already checking tack and tightening cinches, the evil lass from earlier in the day stepped out in front of Shaw.

Tara was not going to be intimidated by this bold lass. "Who is this, Shaw?"

"An old acquaintance—the one who was Dougal's sweetheart some years ago. What do you want, Eschina? Be quick about it. We're leaving."

"I told you what I wanted before. Meet me at

midnight or else."

"Or else what?"

Eschina took a look at Tara and said, "I'm sure she doesn't know everything about your past, does she?"

Shaw took Tara's hand and led her away, ignoring Eschina's parting remarks.

"You'll regret it if you ignore me!"

How Tara wished Riley were here so she could read Shaw's mind. Even Tara could tell he was furious, but she longed to know what exactly had angered him so.

CHAPTER ELEVEN

ONCE MOST OF the household had found their beds that night, Shaw sat in front of the hearth in Marcas's solar waiting for his brothers. Ethan had told Marcas there were stories to be told, and the three had arranged to meet in the solar once the hall was empty.

He couldn't help but tap his foot with impatience. If they didn't show within a quarter hour, then he'd find his own bed. It wasn't like he *wanted* to tell this story. Even—especially?—to his brothers.

If he went to bed, he could dream of sweet lips and the soft skin of Tara Cameron's neck.

Bootsteps came from the direction of the tower room, and Shaw bolted out of his chair. Ethan entered the solar a heartbeat later. "Marcas is not here yet?"

"Nay, but I think I hear him."

Marcas's step sounded on the stone stairs, and he entered the chamber with a solemn nod. He looked every inch the clan chief this night, and Shaw was struck by both pride in his brother and trepidation at the conversation to come. At least they would not be overheard; the bedchambers were all on the opposite end of the castle.

Marcas took a seat behind his desk and leaned back in his chair. Once they were all seated, he said, "Ethan didn't tell me much, but enough to know this is a serious matter, Shaw. Whatever it is, you need to tell the story. Anyone who is blackmailing you for coin will never stop, mayhap not until you or he is dead."

"I cannot disagree with you, Marcas. This situation is escalating, and I don't know what to do anymore." How he hoped his brothers could help him to find a way out of this situation.

"Start at the beginning. Ethan and I will allow you to tell the story without interruption. I promise." Marcas looked over at Ethan to see his reaction.

"I agree." Ethan crossed his arms and waited.

"It has to do with Lucretia Baird's death three years ago. I was there. Dougal was seeing Eschina and I truly liked Lucretia, so we invited them with us for a hunting game Dougal and I often engaged in. We were competitive, see who could kill the most. Loser had to drag all the beasts back to our lands. Lucretia didn't have her own mount, so I took Zinna along for her to ride."

Ethan lifted his hand from the arm of his chair, and he stared at Shaw.

Marcas said, "All right, I'll be the one that will stop you. I should not have promised not to ask questions. Apparently, Ethan feels the same. Go ahead and ask your question, Ethan. Mayhap we have the same one."

Ethan nodded, a look of relief crossing his face. "Eschina was never allowed with a lad unless she had an escort of guards. MacHeth insisted."

"'Tis true. Dougal paid the guards good coin to give us two hours alone, though she was continually sneaking away from them, even without the bribe to look the other way."

"Understood."

Marcas's eyes widened. "That was my question also. The guards agreed? They're lucky they weren't strung up by their bollocks in front of the tower."

"I had naught to do with that and had no objection to the guards. We have had them near before, but for some reason this time, Dougal didn't want them around. However, Eschina wasn't with us for long. We were only about halfway through the hunt when she left. She was mad at Dougal because he'd promised her a picnic, but it never happened. She left when she got hungry and he gave no sign of stopping. Lucretia chose to stay."

Marcas snorted at that. "Dougal is such an arse. Then again, Eschina is used to getting her way. Go on."

"We'd been hunting for about an hour, and Dougal had two deer to my one. We saw a couple of bucks so we went after them. Dougal shot one, so of course, that put the pressure on me. We headed out quickly, Lucretia included, and Dougal went ahead of us, taking a path where we had to jump a fallen tree. I sent my horse sailing over the tree and then forded the stream—you know the place where Kinleigh Burn flows wide and shallow—but Lucretia was afraid. She didn't budge for the longest time, just sitting there shaking her head nay, the wolfhounds barking at her as if to hurry her along. I shouted to her, insisting that she come on and that Zinna could make the jump, so she tried it."

Both brothers let out a sigh, guessing what was coming next.

"What happened?" Marcas asked, his voice low, as if he hated to ask.

"You can guess, I'm sure. Zinna's back leg must have caught on something, and they fell, both landing in the brush. I heard their screams, and out of nowhere came Dougal, as if he'd circled back. He made it to Lucretia's side before I did. He yelled for me to go get the sheriff, that the Cromarty sheriff wasn't far away.

"I still don't know why I left, but I did. By the time I returned, less than a quarter hour later, Dougal held Lucretia's head in his lap and Zinna was dead. I rushed to Lucretia's side and grasped her hand. I told her I was sorry, and she kept trying to talk, but all she could get out was 'Dougal, Dougal.' Then she was gone."

"How did Zinna die?"

"She had two broken legs, so she had to be put down. Dougal did it while I went for the sheriff, and I was grateful. I don't know if I could have done it. And I feel like I killed Lucretia myself by forcing her to take that jump. She was sweet, and she didn't deserve to die so young."

Shaw hung his head; the pain of losing his sweetheart and being partly at fault for her death had haunted him every day since, no matter how hard he'd tried to forget. They hadn't known each other long, because she had only just arrived on Black Isle, but he had enjoyed her company. What might have happened if she had lived? And losing his dear Zinna at the same time had been a near equal blow.

Ethan asked, "Did you find the sheriff?"

"Aye," he answered. "He came a few minutes behind me and said he'd take care of Lucretia's body and tell MacHeth. I didn't know what else to do so I left."

"You just left?" Marcas asked. "That seems cold."

Ethan shook his head. "Nay, that is what I would have done, the shock of the two deaths more than I could handle. In fact, I would have run completely away, unlike Shaw, who probably just rode home."

"I did. I was so distraught that I'd forgotten the deer I'd killed. I went back the next day—the meat would have been no good, but I wanted to bury Zinna—but they were gone. So I did the only other thing I could do. I brought buckets of water from the stream and washed the blood away."

"The animals were all gone, including the horse?"

"Aye, why do you ask?"

"Just curious," Marcas said. "I see it was a devastating event for you. You've said nothing about the blackmail yet. I don't see that the blackmailer had any true guilt to hold over you, though. It seems to have been a tragic accident, no more your fault than Lucretia's or Zinna's, for that matter." Marcas steepled his fingers together on the desk, as he often did when he was thinking harder than usual.

"At the beginning of the following winter, Sammy brought me a note. Some young lad had handed it to him at the market and said it was for me. He never read it, just brought it to me. It said, 'I know what you did, and unless you wish for me to tell everyone you killed the lass, leave gold under the stone beside the kirkyard gate.'" The words of the note were seared onto his memory.

"And you've been paying ever since?"

"Aye, but not only to protect myself. I could bring the shame on our clan. If word had gotten out that I killed her, Papa would have been shamed, and both of you. I cannot sully our clan's honor. How could I allow that to happen? So I paid. Twice a year at first, but of late, the amount and frequency have increased. Dougal is also paying."

"So the story about Lucretia catching a fever and dying is fabricated," Ethan stated for clarification.

"Aye. The lie was told to salvage her reputation. One lass with the two of us, no chaperone or guards around, would not have gone over well with the Chieftain of Clan Baird."

"So the sheriff must be your blackmailer, Shaw. Who else could it be?" Marcas asked. "It has to be someone who can write, and that narrows the list significantly."

"'Tis more than possible, but he's a sheriff—

why wouldn't people believe his version of events? You know how it was with Padraig. The bastard locked him in a cell for no reason and would have been happy to leave him there."

"And Dougal pays too?" Ethan asked. "Exactly the same amount?"

"Aye. Neither of us know what to do about it. I think we're stuck for life."

"What are you afraid of?" Marcas asked. "You didn't kill her, so why not let the truth come out? I understand when Da was alive, as he would have been upset, but I'm not worried about our reputation. Let it go."

Shaw jumped from his chair, his fingers pointed to his own chest. "Because no matter what you say, if this person reveals either Dougal or me as the killer, then the Baird chieftain will come for me and for you. I can't allow you to be implicated in a murder when you've just found happiness, Marcas. And do you think Aedan Cameron will allow his daughter to marry a murderer?"

Marcas arched a brow and broke into a half grin. "So your feelings for Tara are that strong, aye? I think this is driving your actions more than anything. I always believed you had your eye on the lass, from the day we kidnapped her from Cameron land. 'Struth?"

"Aye, I have, but because of this issue, I've tried my best to ignore the draw the lass has on me."

"You cannot fight love, brother," Marcas said.

In the spring, people had started dying on Matheson land, including Marcas's first wife and both parents. In desperation, he and his brothers had kidnapped who they thought were the two best healers in all the land, Jennie Cameron and Brenna Ramsay. Instead, they mistakenly stole their daughters away, and Jennet had willingly come along with Brigid.

It had been the wisest thing Marcas had ever done, though he could perhaps have done it in a better manner. The lasses had saved his daughter and son along with many others.

"'Tis a long time to try to tamp down your feelings," Marcas said.

"I cannot do it any longer. I'm in love with her."

"Have you declared this to her yet?" Ethan asked.

"Nay, I'm still trying to understand it myself, and I have much on my mind between the faerie glen, the blackmailing, and the parents of the lass I'd like to marry arriving without warning."

Marcas chuckled. "I'm loving it all, and you'll find your way out soon enough."

"Will you help me?"

"Of course. Ethan, what say you about everything?"

Their logical brother's contorted expression told them he had something he wished to say.

"So what does Eschina want?" Ethan asked.

The rapid change in topic made Shaw blink in surprise. "She wishes to meet me at midnight. I have no idea what she wants, and I'm not going. She tried to threaten me by mentioning my past in front of Tara, saying something to the effect that she would tell Tara all that happened. But I doubt she knows the truth. I cannot guess what her purpose is."

"Could she have twisted something you said? Or would Dougal have told her the truth? They were seeing each other," Marcas suggested.

"Marcas, I never spoke to Eschina after Lucretia died. Dougal said he lied to her and told her we ended the hunt shortly after she left. She wouldn't know the truth unless the sheriff told her."

Marcas picked up a small figurine on his desk that belonged to their sire, turning it over and over in his hand while he stared at the wall. "Are you sure you trust that Dougal never told her?"

"I do. I don't think Dougal would betray me."

Ethan said, "I must agree with that. If Dougal told Eschina, everyone would know by now. She would tell the tale, exaggerated into an epic saga, just for the sake of seeing everyone's reaction. Besides, she cannot write, so could not be the one sending the notes. I think you must speak with Dougal. The two of you must confront the sheriff."

Marcas nodded. "I can't help but think 'tis the sheriff of Cromarty also. If only the sheriff and Dougal know, who else could it be?"

"It's possible the sheriff shared it with someone we don't even know. What if the other person is doing the work and the sheriff is taking part of our coin? How will we ever know? I have tried following our money drops. Sammy has tried, and Dougal too, but to no avail. We never see anyone pick it up, either at the town stables in Beauly, where I send mine, or the hollow log where Dougal leaves his."

"Someone could definitely be assisting the sheriff in this venture. I agree with Ethan," Marcas said. "You and Dougal need to face him together."

"And there's more." He had to get up and pace a bit before he revealed the next part. Forcing himself to recall the faerie glen, he thought about that beast appearing in front of him.

The unicorn had Zinna's markings. Her size, her mane, the way she whinnied. It was his horse, but whether flesh or spirit, he couldn't say.

"Go on," Marcas persisted.

"I know you'll find this hard to believe, but Tara and Riley went to visit the faerie glen about a sennight ago. They saw a horse, a white horse." Ethan already knew, of course, not that he'd show any reaction anyway, but Shaw saw disbelief on Marcas's face.

"I took Tara there yesterday, and while we were at the upper falls, that same white horse appeared." He closed his eyes, the only way he knew to stop the misting that was fighting to come through. The memories of Lucretia dying in Dougal's arms were just too much. His feelings for Tara were so much stronger and didn't compare, but watching Lucretia die had had a powerful effect on the lad he'd been then.

"And?" Marcas pressed.

"And it was Zinna. I saw her with my own eyes, stroked her neck. I checked the marking on her ear. It was her."

Marcas set the figurine down and leaned

forward. "Someone is jesting with you. Setting you up to force you to give them more money. Make you think you are daft. Someone who knows the marks on your horse and put them on this other animal. Zinna is dead, Shaw."

"Someone might use dye to add markings on a horse, but how could they turn the beast into a unicorn? It had a unicorn's horn, and it wasn't tied on with string nor glued to its head." Shaw stopped his pacing and sat back in his chair, leaning toward his brother, his voice coming out in a whisper. "Do you know what Riley told Tara when they saw the horse the first time?"

"Please tell. I find this topic verra interesting," Ethan said. "Especially because Riley has the reputation of being able to speak with the dead."

"She said the horse spoke to her and said she was chained by lies. That until some truth comes out, she cannot go on as the other animals do."

"And you believe this?" Marcas flipped the figuring in his hand a few more times.

Shaw let out a deep breath, resting his forearms on the desk. "Tara told me they saw a white horse there. And when we went together, the horse appeared again. I don't know what to make of Riley and her beliefs, but I am sure of one thing."

"What is that?" Marcas asked.

"You cannot make a false whinny. The horse I saw was Zinna."

CHAPTER TWELVE

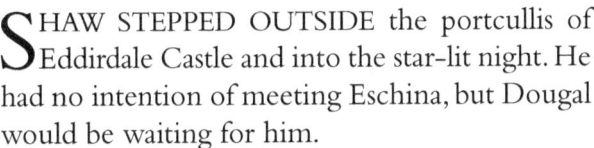

SHAW STEPPED OUTSIDE the portcullis of Eddirdale Castle and into the star-lit night. He had no intention of meeting Eschina, but Dougal would be waiting for him.

He directed his horse through the woods and to the bay, dismounting and moving to the edge of the water. The shore was well lit by the half moon, and the reflection was bright, but clouds skimmed across the sky, covering the moon occasionally. He wasn't there long before Dougal appeared riding down the shore.

"It's just as well you wanted to meet. I know what we said the other day, but I think we must act. Did you have an idea?" Shaw said as soon as Dougal dismounted and joined him at the water's edge, looking over the bay toward Inverness.

"I need to know everything you know. Everything. I think you have been asking lots of questions, and I wish to know how you are approaching this." Dougal looked defeated, his eyes sunken. "What have you learned?"

Shaw sighed and decided to be honest about everything. "Someone is making it worse. I've had enough, Dougal. We need to find out who is doing this and end it."

"I don't know if we can," Dougal replied, crossing his arms and avoiding his gaze.

"Which? Can't stop it or can't find out who is doing it?"

"I doubt if we'll ever find out who the guilty party is. He's too elusive."

"The sheriff is the obvious choice."

"We went over this the other day. The sheriff of Cromarty makes no effort to hide his corruption. It's possible he's paying someone to help, but why would he reduce his take of our coin when there's no reason?"

"Then we'll stop paying, and the culprit will come out of the shadows." Shaw made his declaration and turned to face Dougal. "I didn't do anything wrong other than tell a lass to jump her horse."

Dougal turned to face him. "Are you daft? The lass died! On an outing she shouldn't have been on, one Chief Baird knew naught of. MacHeth guards his womenfolk fiercely, you know that. He'll hang us both by our bollocks and let the ravens pick our eyes out, just for taking them on the hunt without guards. We are both indirectly at fault. He'll see it no other way."

"So what the hell do you suggest we do? I'm not going to give my life's wealth away because of a tragic accident. I'm ready to end this and take our chances."

Dougal's face turned furious, the deep red showing even in the moonlight. "I will not jeopardize my life. My sire will kill me, if MacHeth doesn't. You'll keep your mouth shut about this or I'll come and shut it for you. Now we end these meetings, or someone will overhear. If you think the sheriff is guilty, kill him and be done with it."

"I'll not sink to murder, Dougal. And there's no proof to charge him with."

"Then let it drop and keep your mouth shut and the coin flowing."

Dougal spun around and leaped on his horse, disappearing into the night quicker than Shaw could blink.

He ran his hand down his face, cursing to himself. What a waste of time. Now what? He stared out over the water for a wee bit and was about to leave when another horse came in close, so quietly he barely heard her.

Eschina.

"What the hell do you want?"

"I told you that you would regret it if you didn't meet up with me."

"I have naught to say to you. We haven't spoken in years, so why now of a sudden?" He crossed his arms and glared at her.

She sauntered toward him, her hips swaying provocatively, though she did nothing to stir his loins. "I'm not interested in what you're giving away, Eschina. You can stop your temptress act."

She stopped walking and put her hands on her hips. "Fine. Then listen up. You are courting the Cameron lass. I saw you with her."

"'Tis no concern of yours."

"Mayhap not. But it has been noticed by someone I'm close to. Since you have the Camerons' good regard, you are to learn all you can about the treasure at Lochluin Abbey. I know someone who wants it."

"What are you talking about?" He was cursed for sure. Now someone else was trying to get something from him?

"You will find out all you can and pass it on to me. If she returns home, you'll go with her and spy out the treasure and where it's hidden."

"And if I don't?"

"If you don't, the lie will be out for all to hear." She spun on her boot heel and mounted her horse using a conveniently placed log.

"What lie? What are you talking about?" If he didn't figure this out, he'd rip every hair out of his head.

"We'll tell everyone."

"Tell them what?"

"That you're a murderer."

Tara lay awake in the chamber she shared with Riley. She was still trying to come up with a way to convince her parents that she should stay here, though the near abduction had almost changed her mind. She sighed and stared into the dimness. The half moon granted the room just enough light to reveal the shapes of the furniture around the room.

Riley sat bolt upright in their shared bed and looked straight at her, the look on her face startling in its intensity.

"Tara, you have to leave."

"What?" she asked, leaning up on her elbows.

"Shaw is leaving the castle. Follow him. He's going down to the bay. You can walk."

"Come with me." She thought her sister must still be asleep and dreaming, but what if she wasn't?

"Nay, you must go alone." Riley clutched Tara's hand. "You must go. You will be safe. Hurry, I'll help you dress." She climbed out of bed, clearly awake and lucid. This was no dream, for either of them.

Tara sighed and followed. Tossing her night rail and chemise on the bed, she grabbed a pair of leggings her aunt Gwyneth had made for her, donned a tunic, and fussed with her plait. While she wasn't sure she trusted Riley's prediction, if there was a chance it gave her an excuse to be alone with Shaw, she would take it.

She gave Riley a quick hug after rinsing her mouth out and said, "I'm sure I won't be long, though I have no idea why I'm going."

"Godspeed, sister."

Tara nodded, opening the door to their chamber quietly before tiptoeing out and latching it again. Grateful her parents were housed in the tower, she crept down the staircase, and across the great hall without running into anyone.

She grabbed her mantle from the peg next to the front door but didn't bother putting it on until she was out in the cold, shivering a wee bit. Pausing in the shadow of the castle wall, she took in all that was taking place, looking to see who was out and about, pleased to see it was quiet.

She crept over to the portcullis, surprised to see it was still open, and not surprised to run into Torcall, one of the Matheson guards. He greeted her and pointed. "Shaw took the path to the bay. I'll keep the gate open until he returns. Would you like a horse or an escort?"

"Nay, I'd enjoy the walk. 'Tis a lovely night."

"I'll keep an eye out for any lurking danger, but I can only see you until you're under the trees, so make sure 'tis safe since you'll be alone, especially after what happened to you in Rosemarkie. Shaw should still be there, but if he's not, come straight back."

She nodded and set off at a brisk pace down the path, snuggling inside her mantle and pulling the hood up for warmth. It was a lovely night, the stars shining bright through the occasional cloud. She was nearly there when a horse went flying away from the bay and toward Rosemarkie, a woman in the saddle. Even in the dark, Tara could see the furious look on her face.

Eschina.

She nearly turned around, but she didn't, instead thinking of Riley's urgency. She took some satisfaction from the fact that Eschina had not looked happy. Forcing her feet forward, she moved onto the shore. Shaw stood near the water's edge with his head hanging down.

She stopped when she was a horse's length away from him. "It can't have been good news she brought you."

He lifted his head and spun around, his hand going to the dagger on his belt. But his whole face lit up when he saw her, and at the sight, her heart sang a wee tune.

"What are you doing out here in the middle of the night, Tara? And unescorted?" He moved over to her quickly, wrapping his arms around her. "You're cold."

She shrugged, unwilling to admit her sister had sent her. "Just a hunch. I couldn't sleep. Torcall said you were here, and he kept an eye on me."

"I'm glad you're here. Eschina is trying to threaten me, using something that happened a long time ago to make me do her will." He stared up at the stars in the sky and said, "Mayhap I'll draw strength from the stars to see this through. I've had enough of this blackmail and these fools trying to threaten me." He gazed down at her. "You inspire me to do better, be stronger. For you, lass of mine, I'll put an end to this ridiculous situation. Especially in that cute garment that warms your sweet arse so nicely." He bent close and nipped her ear.

She gave him a shove, and he laughed. "Aunt Gwyneth's leggings are purely practical."

"I'll have to thank your aunt if I ever meet her. You have a lovely bottom."

"Never you mind," she said, narrowing her eyes at him. "Be serious for a wee bit. Does your quandary have something to do with the horse in the faerie glen?"

"Aye." He took her hand and tugged her over to a nearby log in the moonlight. "Sit with me and I'll tell you. This is getting to be too much, even for me."

"All right. I am a good listener." He sat down next to her and leaned over to give her a quick kiss.

"You're that and much more, Tara Cameron."

Her insides nearly turned to mush over that declaration. "I like you too, Shaw."

He cocooned her hand inside his and stared out over the bay. She wanted to give him whatever time he needed to tell his story.

"Three years ago, Dougal and I invited two lasses to go hunting with us. Eschina was going with Dougal, and I invited a relative of hers along who was visiting for the summer. I didn't have any relationship with her like I do with you, but she was a sweet lass."

Tara listened to Shaw's story, dreading how it would end, but she didn't interrupt. He was trusting her with this secret he'd clearly held for far too long, and she would honor that trust by listening carefully. As he described Lucretia's hesitance to jump the fallen tree, her eyes started to prickle with tears.

"Zinna jumped but fell and was seriously injured. We had to put her down to end her suffering. She was my horse—I had loaned her to Lucretia for the outing. She was white, with a quarter-moon marking on her ear."

"How terrible. I'm so sorry, but it does explain much about the horse at the faerie glen. What lies do you think she is referring to?"

Shaw turned to look at her and cupped her

cheek with one hand. "I pray you won't hate me for this. I tell you this in confidence. I've kept it a secret for a long time—I've only just told my brothers—but I must be honest with the lass who means more to me than any other."

"Of course I won't hate you. And I'm verra good at keeping secrets."

His thumb brushed her cheek, but then he dropped his hand, taking hold of hers again. "Lucretia died from the fall too. Dougal sat with her while I went for the sheriff. I don't know exactly how she was injured, but she died in Dougal's arms."

She couldn't hide her gasp. "Did no one know?"

"Nay, the sheriff told her uncle she'd fallen from her horse and didn't mention our names. Eschina's father told Lucretia's father that she died of the fever. Apparently, he wasn't willing to admit the two lasses had snuck away under his watchful eye."

"So what does Eschina want?"

"She's threatening to tell everyone I am a murderer if I don't do as she says. Eschina had left when the accident happened, but apparently her father must have told her about the fall. But Eschina's threats are new. The other we've been paying off for years."

"But you didn't kill anyone. Why do you pay?"

He was sweating in the middle of a chilly night, a sign of his distress over the whole complicated mess. He shook his head from time to time, as if his mind was arguing with itself over all that had happened.

"I know I didn't kill her, but I invited her out and pushed her to attempt the jump. So I do bear some responsibility—though it wasn't murder. But if word got out, even if false, it would sully my clan's name. I feared repercussions from my father, so quickly paid the blackmailer. Damn my sire for instilling such a strong code of honor in all of us."

"But your father is here no more. Does that not change it in your mind?"

"It makes it different. I spoke with my brothers, and Marcas agrees with you, but I don't wish to bring this all on him when he's so happy. Brigid has made him happier than I've ever seen him. I don't wish to bring Clan Baird down upon us, jeopardize our reputation as an honorable clan of Black Isle."

She reached up and ran her fingers through the locks of hair falling on the collar of his mantle, straightening them. "'Tis that code of honor that draws me to you."

He stared at her, and she swore she caught a misting in his gaze. "'Tis the same code that tells me I'm not worthy of you, Tara Cameron. A nobleman's daughter, the daughter of one of the finest healers in all the land, and I'm going to be called a murderer. I'll have no chance of ever making you mine."

She pulled him down and kissed his lips softly. "I'm yours when you do want me. I know what's true and in your heart, and that is what is most important. Not the lies of others."

He kissed her tenderly, tugging her onto his lap

and slanting his mouth over hers to deepen the kiss. Tara's heart soared. How she loved the taste of this man, the feeling of being in his arms, the wonder of every new experience with him. Just a look from him could set butterflies aflight deep in her belly.

She touched his face, reveling at the roughness of his beard, drinking in more of him with every angle and touch of his tongue.

He ended the kiss and stared into her eyes. "I have to right all of this before I can ask you to be mine. I promise you I will fix this so when I ask for your hand in marriage, your father will have no reason to reject me. Will you wait for me, lass?"

"I will. I will always wait for you, Shaw."

CHAPTER THIRTEEN

TARA SAT ACROSS from her mother at the trestle table the next morning. Her father and Brin had just gone out to the stables to chat with the Mathesons. Brigid was feeding the bairns with Nonie's help, and Jennet was cutting linen strips for new bandages.

Riley hadn't risen yet.

"Do you think Riley is ill, Aunt Jennie?" Jennet asked. "'Tis unusual for her to be sleeping so late."

Her mother shook her head while swallowing her bite of porridge. "Riley often sleeps on an odd schedule. Sometimes her dreams are not restful. Being a seer has its challenges."

"Does she speak with the dead often?" Brigid asked.

"Nay, not often, and I'm glad of it. 'Tis a task that exhausts her. Was she awake when you came down, Tara?"

"Nay, she was still sound asleep. She did have a restless night." She didn't add that she was as exhausted as Riley from her late-night interlude with Shaw. She was so pleased with the words and kisses they'd exchanged in the moonlight, she had been too excited to sleep.

She was beginning to understand exactly why Brigid had married so quickly. The Matheson men had a way of drawing lasses in and holding them tight. Had she fallen in love with her own Matheson?

Her mother had once told her and Riley that she'd know a man was right for her when he made her heart sing whenever he entered the hall. Shaw had been making her heart sing for weeks now, but with all that had happened around them, they hadn't had the opportunity to indulge in spending much time together.

The curse, the witchery accusation against Jennet, the battle with the MacKinnies. So much had happened on Black Isle, and it had been quite nice to have everything calm for a bit.

If only they could settle the issues of that horse, Eschina, and the ongoing blackmail. If she was fretting this much over it, how much worse must it be for Shaw and Dougal?

Was it possible Eschina wanted Shaw for herself and was somehow trying to win his affection?

She chided herself for not having faith in Shaw. He had no interest in Eschina, so jealousy on her part, no matter how beautiful the other woman, was uncalled for and childish. She knew she had a stronger hold on Shaw Matheson's heart than Eschina did.

But this whole situation of the horse and the lass who died had them both unsettled.

"Tara, have you returned with Riley to the faerie glen to see if that horse returned?" Jennet asked.

She shook her head, then decided to be completely honest, especially since her sire wasn't here to toss his looks of disapproval her way. "Nay, not with Riley, but I took Shaw there two days ago."

"And?" her mother pried quietly.

"And a white horse did come out to greet us when we went up to the second waterfall. It was standing in the pool at the base of the falls." She thought again and continued, "It was the same, a white unicorn."

Brigid gave a little squeal. "Truly? The same horse?" Then she leaned toward Tara and said, "And a unicorn too. I love it!"

"Aye, it was a true unicorn, with a majestic spike coming out between her eyes. She looked quite regal to me. But she wasn't pure white—she had a moon-shaped mark under one ear."

Nonie looked to Brigid and said, "That sounds like Shaw's mare, Zinna."

"We think it is, Nonie."

A scream shattered their conversation. Riley flew along the balcony, her head twisting back and forth, her hair wild and unplaited. She leaned over the railing, her screams turning to sobs quickly.

"Riley!" her mother shouted. "Stop where you are!"

Tara bolted from her seat and ran up the stairs to see if she could pull her sister back to the present world and out of her dream, whatever it was. She'd never seen her sister so distressed and wild.

She grabbed Riley's hands and tugged. "Riley, wake up!" She shook her hands with no result, then grabbed her shoulders while her mother stood beneath the balcony shouting up at them.

The door banged open, and her father and brother raced in. Brin took the stairs two at a time and grasped Riley's shoulders, turning her from Tara to face him.

He gripped her chin in one hand. "Riley. Wake up now."

Tears soaked Riley's cheeks, and her screams subsided to sobs as she stared at her brother, collapsing against him. He was a foot taller than his sister, and he bore all her weight without difficulty.

Tara's heart broke, watching them. Why had Riley been given such an odd gift? She couldn't help but wonder what kind of dream had caused such an outburst, unlike any she'd ever seen before. Brin, so tall and strong, held her tight while she calmed, her head resting on his shoulder.

"Come, we'll go downstairs and see Mama and Papa. You can sit by the fire, warm the chill from your bones," Brin said softly.

Tara hurried down the staircase to a basket of furs near the hearth, grabbing one to cover Riley's shoulders as soon as she reached the bottom of the staircase.

Riley stopped moving when her gaze settled on Tara. She froze mid-step, her eyes widening.

Everyone else froze with her.

"Tara, we must go," Riley said, her voice hoarse

from her screams.

"What?" Tara asked, totally confused.

"Go where and why, Riley?" her father asked from behind Tara. "What did you see in your dream?"

"I saw them." Riley appeared to be in a trance, her gaze seeing but not anything in front of her.

Tara hated this part of Riley's dreams. Often it took half the hour to learn all the details from them. Riley had told her once she had to sift through all the images in her mind to come up with the right explanation.

"Saw who?" Brin asked. "Who did you see?"

"The people. The ones trying to hurt her."

"Hurt who?"

Her finger came up to point to Tara, then her hand came back to her mouth, covering her sob. "Tara."

No one spoke. What in the Lord's name had she dreamed? Tara moved closer and whispered. "Riley? Are you sure? Think hard."

"And tell us who's trying to hurt her, lass. Who did you see?" her father persisted, stepping closer.

"Four of them. Three men and a lass surrounded you."

"What was Tara doing?" Brin squeezed her shoulders. "You're almost there. Finish the dream for us."

Shaw opened the door and stepped inside, Ethan and Marcas directly behind him. All three froze in the doorway. Tara would have moved to him, but her feet were frozen to the spot in the middle of the hall.

Riley closed her eyes and sagged against her brother. "They killed you, Tara. All of them. All were part of it."

Tara stared at her sister, unable to believe what she'd just said.

"I watched you die."

CHAPTER FOURTEEN

SHAW GASPED, NEARLY choking over Riley's declaration. Was it supposed to be a prediction? Would her family believe her without a doubt?

If he didn't know Tara and Riley so well, he never would have believed it. And even so, he wasn't sure what to make of the scene before him. Riley seemed to be barely present. He'd never heard of anyone besides her who had dreams of what was to come. It was such an eerie sensation to watch the family interact with her in such a trance-like state. But even more shocking was her declaration.

The Cameron men had been halfway back to the castle when they'd started to run. Shaw had looked to his brothers, knowing by the way the visitors were acting that something important had happened. They all dropped what they were doing and followed. They were already on their way when Brigid stuck her head outside and called to them.

"Marcas! Shaw! Hurry!"

Ethan, always the quickest, reached the door

first, but Shaw was directly behind him and moved him to the side. Ethan asked, "What is it, Brigid?"

"Tara. Riley. I don't know. Hurry."

Shaw had no idea what she meant, but he hadn't waited to find out.

Riley leaned against her brother, sobbing uncontrollably. Jennie and Aedan Cameron weren't far away, but they didn't interfere, and the others hovered at the periphery of the circle they formed.

After Riley finished explaining the dream she saw, Tara shrank back with slow, painful steps that told him just how completely she did believe her sister. Unconcerned about how her parents would react, he moved to her side immediately, taking her shoulders to turn her away from Riley.

"Tara, do not worry, I'll protect you." The fear and confusion in her face nearly ripped his heart out. Ach, he loved this woman, and it near killed him to see her hurting.

"Tara? Talk to me. Please." He moved his hand to cup her face, and she finally brought her gaze to his. "It does not have to be true. She can tell us who she saw, and we'll know who to go after. This could prove to be verra helpful."

Her father tried to push his hand away, but he wouldn't allow it. "Tell me exactly what you believe to be true."

Tara gripped his other hand with her own and said, "Riley dreamed my death, and I believe her. She's often correct, Shaw."

He had to consciously close his jaw, which

had dropped open in shock. There were so many questions darting around in his mind, he didn't know what to focus on. "Has she had dreams like this before? Tell me exactly what she saw. I didn't hear everything."

All he wished to do was wrap his arms around Tara and hide her away from everyone and everything.

Jennet came over to them and said, "Riley dreamed that four people were trying to kill Tara. Three men and a lass. Whether they are successful is yet to be proven, but we must pay attention to what she says. Ignoring her could be dangerous. Any suspicions as to who they could be?"

Ethan came up behind Jennet and arched a brow at Shaw. "I think we all know who the lass is, but the identities of three men are still in question."

Jennet leaned forward and whispered into Tara's ear. Shaw just caught the words. "Eschina. It must be."

Shaw said, "Can she tell you who they are, Tara? What they look like?"

Tara leaned against him and said, "I'll ask her more once she's calmer." Tara took a deep, shuddering breath, then another calmer one. Then she stepped away from him and sought out her sister. Brin had settled Riley in a chair in front of the fire, covering her with furs while her mother brought her a cup of broth to drink.

Aedan Cameron wasn't to be waylaid. "Marcas, I'll see you and Shaw in your solar now."

Tara said, "I'm coming too."

"Aye, you should come too, Tara." Her father gave her a quick nod as he headed toward the stairs.

Marcas kissed Brigid's cheek and led the group to his solar. Aedan stopped for a moment and turned to Tara's mother. "We're leaving as soon as Riley's condition allows, but no later than the morrow." Then he gave Tara a look that told Shaw exactly how much the man loved his daughter. He'd not often seen that kind of sadness and vulnerability in a commanding chieftain. "Tara, you're coming home with us. No arguments."

Tara didn't answer, just moved with the group toward the solar. Shaw fell into step with her and wrapped his arm around her shoulders, anything to try to stop the poor lass's shaking.

What the hell was happening?

Once the door to the solar had closed behind them, Aedan took charge. "I need to know who you suspect the four people to be. And no lying or deceit. Marcas?"

Marcas sat in his chair, indicating for the others to sit, then looked to Shaw. "I don't think we can answer that question, but I'll let Shaw explain what he knows and what he suspects. Shaw?"

Shaw cleared his throat, sifting through his thoughts and trying to decide where to start. The white horse? Eschina? The sheriff?

A unicorn?

He wasn't sure who the three men could be. So he'd start with what he did know. "The lass I'm quite sure about. Eschina MacHeth came to me last eve and told me I was to go to Lochluin

Abbey with Tara when you return home. She wants me to get information about the abbey's treasure. Apparently word has traveled to Black Isle about the wealth of Lochluin Abbey and the Cameron connection with the abbey. I refused, of course, and she left angry. But she threatened to spread some lie about my past if I didn't help."

Aedan leaned back in his chair and said, "I'll accept that, but tell me why this lass thinks she could have any hold over you, Shaw. What is this lie she spoke of? If you're going to marry my daughter, I need to know all."

Tara said, "Papa, please. Do not embarrass me."

Shaw reached for her hand and said, "Aye, I am verra attached to your daughter, but I need to sort out a few things in my life before I would ask you for her hand. I intend to do just that, my lord, and I hope it to be soon. Eschina refused to say more beyond her vague threat. I am being honest when I tell you that I don't know who the other three men are."

Marcas said, "Shaw, tell him everything. 'Tis no time for secrets. 'Tis time for this to be out in the open. Chief Cameron has more experience in these kinds of situations than we do, I am sure. His advice could prove invaluable."

Shaw sighed and glanced at Tara who gave him a nearly imperceptible nod. "I made a mistake in my youth that I am still paying for. I have been blackmailed for over two years now, and I am still unable to determine who is behind it. I've spoken to a friend who is also being victimized with the hope of seeking out the guilty party, but he refuses to join me in this. If I stop paying, he suffers the consequences as well, so 'tis not an easy choice."

Aedan crossed his hands in his lap. At one point, Shaw had thought Tara looked just like her mother, but looking into this man's eyes was much like looking into Tara's. His brown hair was still full, though gray peppered his long locks, giving him a distinguished appearance.

Perhaps Marcas was correct and this man could assist him in finding a solution.

"Shaw, I understand the poor judgment of young lads, but if you wish for my assistance, you must tell me all."

Shaw glanced at his brother, wishing to make certain Marcas agreed, and he clearly did. And so for the third time in less than a day, he told the story of the hunt and its tragic ending, the loss of a horse and worse, a lass just setting out in life.

"And the blackmailer is threatening both you and your friend?"

"Aye, but we receive separate notes and pay separately. The blackmailer threatens to say that I murdered the lass. It didn't happen that way. I went for the sheriff while my friend stayed with her. She took her last breath moments after I returned."

Aedan stood up and held his hand out to Tara.

"Tara, go pack your and Riley's things. Shaw, you'll not be marrying my daughter until this matter is settled. I'll not put her life at risk anymore. I don't know if this or the lass's wish to plunder the abbey is connected to whoever hired that man to kidnap Tara, but it seems too likely to discount. We are verra worried about the safety of both of our daughters." He nodded to Marcas and said, "I thank you for your hospitality."

The two headed to the door, Tara glancing back over her shoulder with tears in her eyes, and Shaw was nearly undone.

"My lord," he called, rising from his chair and standing tall.

The Cameron chieftain turned around and lifted his chin. His broad shoulders filled the doorway.

Shaw said, "I'm going with you. I insist on protecting Tara until she is safely on Cameron land. 'Tis my honor and my duty."

A slow smile crept across the Cameron's face. "If you didn't, you'd never see her again. And I insist on it if you wish for my help."

"Aye, my lord." Shaw was so relieved by the man's words that his knees nearly buckled.

"We'll find the bastards who dare to threaten my daughter. All four of them," the clan chieftain said. "You can count on it."

CHAPTER FIFTEEN

TARA SHIVERED INSIDE her mantle, glad they'd finally arrived on Cameron land. They'd left early the day after Riley's dreams, and it was now the next evening. Darkness would fall soon. Lochluin Abbey was up ahead, proof she was finally home.

Safe.

"I'm grateful you came along," she said to Shaw, who rode abreast of her. "I hope you'll stay a few days before you return. I would like to show you my home."

"It is my duty and pleasure to see you home safely, and if I'm welcome, I'd like to stay until we can decipher Riley's dream." He glanced over at her, waggled his eyebrows the way he often did, and smiled.

She smiled back. Even in the near dark of a gloomy day, he was the handsomest man around, and his smile melted her heart.

"I will protect you, Tara, with my verra life if I must. I know we haven't discussed Riley's dream, but surely everything she dreams doesn't come true."

She nodded. She'd thought of that exact possibility over and over in the last few days. "She believes we can prevent the things her dreams foreshadow." She peered ahead at her sister, who was riding between Brin and her father. The score of guards they had brought along surrounded their whole party, and she was glad to have them. "I choose to believe she is correct."

"Then I will believe it, as well." Shaw gestured with his chin at the soaring stone structures ahead of them. "Is that the abbey?"

"Aye. 'Tis one of the few double abbeys. It houses both nuns and monks who work tirelessly transcribing documents. The chapel itself is beautiful, with tall arches throughout. As a child, they looked to me as if they touched the sky. I will take you there to see up close, because it is beautiful. And I'll show you the hill behind the abbey where my mother and father spent time staring up at the stars."

"Staring at the stars?"

She loved to tell this story about her parents, because she thought it oddly romantic.

Many people thought her father's interests odd, but her mother wasn't among them, just one of the many reasons he adored her. In return, her mother had a special cottage built for them behind their castle just to be alone. "My father is verra interested in astrology. He studies the shapes and formations of the stars in the night sky. Reads everything he can about it. He loves astrology the way my mother loves learning about healing and anatomy. And he loves my mother even more than he loves astrology. I know he would go to the ends of the earth for her. He once ordered a fabulous gift for her that upset half the thieves in all the land. It came from Europe in an unusual shipment."

"What kind of gift?"

"Oh, everyone had their own idea of what it could be—a chest of rare gems or exotic spices—but when everyone saw it, the only one who appreciated it was my mother."

"Truly? How could that be?"

"Do you read and write?"

"I read well, but I have much to learn. I consider my writing skills to be rudimentary."

"My grandmother decreed that all the lasses in the clan must learn how to read and write, thus, I love to read. I am fortunate that I have a place like the abbey, which is full of books. 'Tis a topic for another day. Allow me to explain my father's gift to my mother. It was paper, a material for writing on like parchment, but made of wood rather than animal skin. 'Tis lighter and thinner. And he's since found her special writing implements. Some are kept here in Mama's healing chamber."

"Why did he wish to buy her something other than parchment? Is that not what everyone uses?"

"She keeps records of everyone she sees and what she tries when she's healing. That way she knows what works and what doesn't. Some sicknesses she only sees once a year or so. She says there are too many to remember. Her grandfather taught her to write everything down. My aunt Brenna does too. The paper is easier to store and carry."

"So 'tis precious, but it isn't worth anything? I don't understand."

"My father was courting my mother, so after it arrived from Europe, he had it brought to Grant Castle, set it on a trestle table to show all her brothers and sister. When she opened the twined package safely ensconced in a crate, they each picked up a piece of it. They smelled it and looked it over, but mostly groaned and walked away, so the story goes. All said they'd prefer a new sword."

"Except your mother."

"Exactly. They have the kind of marriage I want. They share their interests and encourage each other. In return for the paper, my mother had some carpenters build a small cottage behind our castle where they could go alone. The roof over their bedchamber can be lifted so they can see the stars from their bed."

"'Tis quite a story, Tara. My thanks for sharing. But even though he likes the stars, he must be a hell of a swordsman to be able to protect the abbey for so long. No one has ever breached the cellars, have they, though the wealth of the abbey is legendary and must tempt thieves across the Highlands. Eschina is daft, in my thinking."

"Some have tried, but they've always been caught. My mother speaks of it as the Lord protecting what is His. But as for my father being a great swordsman…" She leaned over and whispered, "He's not, though he's skilled enough at need. He's more cunning. He prefers trickery to battle skills."

Shaw grinned. "Hmmm. Mayhap I need to have a long conversation with him, learn some of his methods."

"'Tis the way of it in our allied clans. Uncle Alex and his sons are the swordsmen. Uncle Logan and his clan are the archers. Papa is the trickster. Beware."

They drew near the abbey, and all quieted out of respect as they passed. The cross at the peak of the church reached far into the sky, and it was Tara's favorite part because it was so majestic. The two buildings were connected by a passageway. The larger structure included the church and the nuns' living quarters. The monks lived and worked in the other. Two guards stood at attention on the road that turned off to the holy site, and they raised their hands in greeting as the Camerons rode by.

Once they'd passed the abbey, Tara explained, "Papa provides and trains the abbey guards, but Uncle Ruari does much of the daily oversight of the guards, as Papa's second."

They were nearly home when her father slowed his horse and pulled abreast of Shaw. Keeping his voice low, he said, "You know we've been followed, aye?"

Tara's eyes widened, but her sire gave her a look that told her she was to act as if she didn't know, so she looked forward again and said nothing.

Who would be following them?

Shaw gave him a nearly imperceptible nod. "Aye, I noticed. I don't know who it is—they've been very careful to stay hidden—but I can circle back and find out."

"Nay, we'll continue on as if we don't suspect. I have a plan, and I'll explain once we are inside. We'll meet in my solar."

"Agreed. I'll do whatever you suggest, my lord."

Aedan smiled, a sneaky grin that told him the man was indeed fond of trickery. "We'll catch some of the culprits in my web on the morrow."

Tara let out a deep breath. She had to pray that her father was right and they would catch four people, because if they didn't, she wasn't sure if she'd ever be able to sleep again.

CHAPTER SIXTEEN

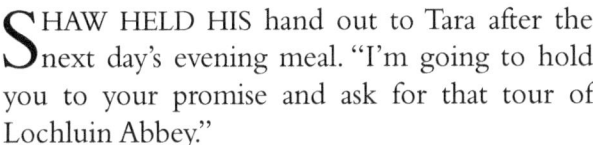

SHAW HELD HIS hand out to Tara after the next day's evening meal. "I'm going to hold you to your promise and ask for that tour of Lochluin Abbey."

She took his hand, the warmth of hers setting heat into his own. "Why, I would love to show you. 'Tis the perfect time because after our tour, it will be dark. I'll introduce you to my father's favorite constellations."

How he wished to nibble her neck or set his hands upon her waist and tug her closer, but he was ever mindful of being in her home, under her parents' watchful eyes. He'd not risk alienating them. Or having the abbess chase him with a broom.

Tara bent to kiss her mother on the cheek. "We'll be back, Mama."

"Do not forget to travel with your guards, lass," her mother added.

"Of course." Tara nodded but shot Shaw a smile as soon as they moved away.

Her uncle Ruari had said he'd serve as their guard, with a couple of others, but he'd promised to keep his distance with a wink and a whisper. "You need a lad in your life, Tara. You've nearly passed the age of marriage."

She nodded to him as she passed him. Shaw held the door to the castle's courtyard open for her.

They chose their mounts, and a pair of stable lads tacked the horses for them and led them into the golden glow of the sunset.

Shaw set his hands on Tara's waist and asked, "May I?"

"Aye, please assist me."

He boosted her into her saddle and couldn't help but let his hand linger on her hip before he moved to his own mount. He didn't dare indulge in any other contact. Anyone could be watching them.

They set off at a brisk pace up the well-worn path across the meadow between the abbey and Cameron Castle. She laughed as the wind loosened her hair from its bindings, until eventually she reached up and took the leather ties away, letting it fly freely.

Tara's beauty only grew in the crisp autumn air, especially when she tipped her head back to look up at the just-appearing stars in the darker eastern sky. "Do you know of the planets? If not, I'd love to point them out to you."

He tipped his head back just as a few clouds interrupted their view. "I've heard some. You can tell me more later. We'll look from the hill later, lass. As your parents did before us. Tell me more about the treasure of Lochluin. Have you seen it?"

"The treasure of the abbey is mostly coin, I believe, though I've not seen it all. It comes from years and years of tithing and weddings and whatever else the monks and nuns do. Payments come from many, so the nuns always told me. They used to say the biggest gifts come from those with the most guilt. They hope to buy their way into Heaven. But I've also seen golden idols and marble statues sent from other lands. The number of silver crosses alone must be higher than I can count. I've also heard of many rubies and emeralds."

They reached the abbey quickly, and Uncle Ruari led them to the stables, though he stayed mounted while Shaw helped Tara down from her horse.

The stable lad said, "The abbess is awaiting you inside. Will you be staying long?" Tara's father had sent word ahead, so their visit would not be a surprise.

Shaw said, "Probably an hour or two. She's promised to give me a tour of the abbey and the cellars."

Ruari bent down to clap Shaw on the shoulder. "Be alert. 'Tis quite a treasure in the cellars. They keep it well protected behind multiple locked doors, but 'tis much like a maze to get to it. You'll not get in to see the treasure, but following the labyrinth of secret tunnels and odd keyrings is verra interesting. 'Tis like a jumbled web."

Shaw had to admit he was more than excited to see exactly what was housed in the cellars—the web of doors and corridors he'd heard described fascinated him. He found it exhilarating to be searching for a treasure. He truly had no wish to see the treasure itself; just seeing where it was housed was enough for him. He gazed up at the sky again. "Perhaps I can take some ideas home to Eddirdale Castle, to keep our own valuables safe. We'll keep the wine at the center of a puzzle to stop anyone who's already had too much from getting more."

Ruari laughed. "We'll be patrolling the area. If you are in any need, we'll be within earshot. Holler and one of us will hear you. I'll leave two guards by the front entrance."

Shaw could barely contain his excitement. Being with Tara alone, looking for treasure. He could think of no better way to pass the time.

He led her over to the door and held it open for her. "The door is always open? Even at night?"

"Aye, just the outer door of the kirk, so one can go into the chapel. They are always willing to house someone in need for the night, and they welcome many visitors." They stood in a small front room, the cozy chapel off to the left. The setting sun struck its stained-glass window, throwing splashes of color across the floor. Tara pointed at the door directly across from them. "That door will be locked. The abbess will join us shortly."

As promised, the door opened a few moments later, and a rotund woman in dark robes came through it, a wide smile on her face. "Greetings to you, sweet Tara. We have not been blessed with your presence in a long time. How do you fare?"

Tara bobbed a short curtsey to the abbess and said, "Verra well, thank you. Mother Mary, this is my friend Shaw Matheson from Black Isle. I have been visiting his clan for a few months, and he was kind enough to see me home. He was hoping for a tour of the abbey before he has to return."

"Of course. 'Tis a pleasure to meet any friend of Tara's. Welcome to Lochluin Abbey, Lord Matheson. Tara knows her way around so well that I'll grant her the privilege of giving you the tour. She's been chasing around these passageways for many years. She and her family are always a delight to have."

"Many thanks to you, Mother Mary," Tara said. "We shall move right along so we are not here too late into the night. Then we hope to look at the stars from your hill."

She clasped her hands together in front of her and said, "Just as your lovely parents did many years ago. I've heard the tale many times. What a beautiful idea. For now, I shall return to my library. If you are in need of anything, you know where to find me."

"Many thanks to you, Reverend Mother," Shaw said.

They stepped farther into the building, into a hall between the foyer and the church proper. The abbess went one direction while he and Tara went the opposite way, down a long passageway that had the highest ceilings he'd ever seen, the sounds of their steps echoing on the stone floor.

Tara pointed above their heads. "I love the different depictions of God and the angels hung on the walls."

"You said this is a double abbey?" Shaw stared up at the high arches as they walked. At the end of the hall, they reached a small doorway and a less-expansive passageway beyond it.

"Aye. This passageway connects the area where the nuns live to where the monks live and work. We'll come back this way to get to the cellars."

They headed down the passageway until they stepped into a beautiful area with tall arched ceilings, even higher than in the chapel, gracefully symmetrical with the appearance of touching the sky. The arches rose into a columnated dome, resplendent with ornate stone structures that looked like large openings but were strictly decorative.

Their path ran along the building with open archways on the other side. "This is the area around the cloister in the monastery." Moving to a door in the side, she opened it and tugged him through it and out into a garden. The landscaping was precise and elegant, the beds separated by walkways paved in flat stone. A few of the garden plants were still green, but many of the beds were empty now, late in the year. "Riley and I used to play here, tag and hide-and-seek. That part of the building," she pointed to the right, "is where the monks live. One of my favorite places, mostly because my mama loves it so, is the scriptorium."

"A scriptorium? I've not heard that word."

"Here," she said, tugging him through another

door. "I'll show you. 'Tis at the end of this hall, but we must be quiet when we approach."

Her command puzzled him, and he followed, curious about where she led him.

"The scriptorium is part of the library, and 'tis where the monks copy texts for royalty and for the church, prayers, science and medical texts, histories, and scripture." She opened a door, and they stepped inside.

There were about eight monks inside, each at their own desk or table hard at work, and most lifted their head in a greeting to her. Each desk held two candles so they could continue to work, though most were reading at this point rather than transcribing. She waved and they returned the greeting, most with a smile, though two never acknowledged them.

She leaned close to Shaw and whispered, "I know most of them, but we won't interrupt their work."

They continued down the passageway again while Tara described the life of the abbey. "There's an infirmary and a small hall with a few beds for travelers or visitors. Then the kitchens are in the back. Mostly they eat verra simply, but for our local festivals, they create wonderful food. My mother always sends baskets of fruit tarts at the holidays for whoever is in residence. They adore her treats. The nuns' dormitory is on the far side of the church in the main building, and there are some small chambers in the cellars. My cousin Connor's wife stayed here for weeks with her daughter. They treated her wonderfully, and she will be forever grateful to them."

At that point, they'd traveled the perimeter of the cloister and were back where they had started.

"It seems a welcoming place, and I'm certain it's a good life for those who feel called to it," Shaw said. He couldn't imagine himself living here— for surely he would always be breaking the rules and missing his prayers in favor of the hunt or a festival or lass. This lass beside him, most likely.

"Aye, I believe so. Joining the order is no light decision, though. I would not be suited to it, myself. It was a wonder they allowed Riley and me to run through the passageways, squealing most of the time. Let us head into the cellars, and I'll show you the mazes and all the protection they have for the treasure."

"Is the only entryway through the abbey?"

"Nay, there are two other entrances, one from the garden and another from outside the main building on the opposite side. They designed it so workers did not have to traipse all the way through the abbey or the monastery. They could just go straight down the staircase and into the cellars. However, this has also caused problems. There have been some who have tried to creep in straight through the back cellar, thinking they could find the treasure on their own. They are often hopelessly lost in the mazes below."

"I canna wait to see it. Lead on, beautiful lady."

She grinned, and her entire face lit up. He loved that Tara didn't try to hide her emotions. Both his brothers were difficult to read from a look, Ethan especially. After all the years he'd spent trying to interpret Ethan's behaviors and expressions, it was pleasing to not have to guess.

He made a point not to be so inscrutable, and he welcomed Tara's openness.

They made a turn at the end of the passageway, then headed down the staircase, well-lit with torches high on the wall. At the bottom, Tara pointed the direction she wished to go.

"Down this way to the center of the cellars, where there is an open chamber. That's where the maze begins. It's quite easy to find your way on this side. The other side is too confusing."

She tugged on his hand, but he tugged her back against him in a shadowed corner, his lips finding hers and devouring her. He knew he couldn't do much in the cellar of an abbey, but he just needed one taste, one reminder of how good they were together, one reminder of the hope he had for their future. At first, he ravaged her lips, but then he cupped her cheeks and softened the kiss before ending it, leaning his forehead against hers.

"How I wish things were different, lass. If I were free to do what I wished, I'd marry you today and hold you in my arms every night and every morn. I'm yours, Tara Cameron, and no force on God's green earth could change that."

"I feel the same. You are the only one for me, Shaw," her voice came out in a husky whisper.

He kissed her lips again, then her forehead and said, "Lead the way. I wish to see this secret path."

Keeping her close by his side, they traveled down the dark corridor, a brighter light now visible at the end. "So this is the center?"

"Aye. From here it becomes a maze."

"Are you certain you remember how to get us out of it?"

She chuckled. "Of course I do. Riley and I were forever hiding from Brin and Uncle Ruari down here."

"Smart to travel with your sister. If you were ever lost, she'd use her special skills to find a way out."

"I'm verra good with directions, so I could find our way out." She stepped into the center area. Four doors led out of it, the one they'd come through, one straight ahead, and one on either side.

He looked at the three choices they had and asked, "Which way?"

She was about to step into the one directly across from them when two hooded monks came through it, nodded to them, and moved on to another passageway.

"They don't speak?" Shaw whispered, not wanting to insult them.

"Some do," she said, "but many spend their days praying, reciting scripture, or reading. I never asked because my mother said it was rude, but I think it depends on their devotion. The ones who work in the scriptorium talk sometimes. Those who keep their hoods raised are the silent ones."

"Are we following those two?"

"Nay, we're going down the passageway they came from. They do check the area near the treasure several times a day. 'Tis probably why they are down here."

They entered the maze, coming to intersection after intersection. Tara chose her way with confidence, never slowing to consider her options, right, left, or straight ahead. Finally they reached a large, well-lit chamber with four doors in the opposite wall.

"The treasure is behind one of those doors." Then she whispered, "I suspect our visitors will be joining us soon."

The sound of footsteps came from behind them, so Shaw spun around, placing himself between Tara and whoever was coming. He guessed three people by the sound of their steps. He felt a twinge of disappointment—he'd been hoping for four, as in Riley's dream. He'd left his sword with his horse out of respect for the abbey, and he'd had no idea how uncomfortable that would make him. They had expected this exact situation, but he still was unsettled without his sword and his fingers twitched to grasp the absent hilt.

He drew his dagger and held it in his right hand, just in case.

"Shaw, put it away. If it's the monks returning, they'll be offended."

The group came into view at a bend in the corridor, and Shaw thought he recognized the man who led the way. Confirmation, then. The person behind him looked to be female in shape, though dressed in breeches. As they came closer, he was certain he'd been right.

The sheriff of Cromarty stepped into the room. "Aye, put the dagger away or we'll kill your wee friend. You can watch as we do it."

Shaw pushed Tara farther behind him just as Eschina came out of the shadowed passageway.

"You are surprised?" she asked. "Nay, I think not. I just neglected to tell you that I would follow you instead of await your return to Black Isle. But many thanks to you, Shaw," she said. She held her own dagger at the ready. "I knew you'd come around to helping. Now put the dagger away."

Shaw and Tara were backed into a corner. A second man, this one carrying a sword, followed Eschina, and they were well and truly outnumbered.

The sheriff took a torch down from the wall. "Drop your knife or I'll set your lass's pretty hair on fire."

The bastard had been guilty all along, and he'd known it. Why had he waited to do something about it? All three moved closer to them, and Tara shrank behind Shaw's large frame. He could feel her hands fisting the back of his tunic and her head against his back.

The unknown guard, who looked like someone had punched him and broken his nose, came closer, the point of his weapon at Shaw's neck. Though Shaw's arms were longer than the other man's, the sword more than made up for his shorter reach. Shaw's dagger was useless.

Tara peeked around his arm and said, "We'll give you what you want and then you can leave. We promise not to tell."

"We'll worry about that in a moment. I haven't decided what to do with you yet." The sheriff glared at her.

"You'll not get the treasure if you touch a hair on Tara's head. This is between you and me, Sheriff. Leave her out of this." Shaw spit on the sheriff's foot.

"I'll tell you how this goes. First you'll fetch us the treasure." The sheriff's narrow gaze told Shaw he was already conniving and planning, the rotten piece of shite.

Tara stood strong and said, "We'll show you the treasure under one condition."

"You're in no position to bargain," the sheriff remarked.

"If you kill us, you'll never get the treasure, so I think we are," Tara shot back. "If you think you can get to it on your own from this point, you're wrong. But it would please me to watch you try."

Shaw shrugged to the three would-be thieves. "Do you think you are the only ones who ever thought they could just walk into the abbey from the back entrance and steal away all their treasure?"

Eschina cast a nervous glance at the sheriff, then said, "What is it you want, Tara Cameron?"

"We'll give you the treasure if you agree to stop blackmailing Shaw and Dougal."

"Blackmailing?" the sheriff asked, looking confused. "Are you blackmailing them, Eschina? You could, I suppose. That entire episode with Lucretia was a shameful thing, to be sure, Shaw, but 'tis not me."

Eschina shook her head. "I'm not blackmailing you. What are they getting from you? Coin? Are they threatening to tell all about Lucretia's death? Tell the world 'tis all your fault?"

"But it isn't his fault," Tara said. "He didn't cause the fall nor cause her injuries. 'Twas an accident, plain and simple."

"Enough delay. 'Tis easy to meet your demand. We promise not to blackmail you, since neither of us have done so to begin with. We have only one goal. Open the door to the treasure, Tara, or we kill Shaw right now." The sheriff switched places with the other fool. "The treasure or death. Your choice."

CHAPTER SEVENTEEN

TARA THOUGHT SHE might heave all over them, but she didn't have time to be sick, so she did what she could to calm her churning belly. "Eschina, my sire has plenty of coin to give you if you just promise to leave us alone."

"'Tis not enough!" The sheriff snarled. "Stop stalling and open the door."

Tara moved over to the second door and opened it.

"What the hell? I didn't need your help if it was that easy."

"There's no treasure here." She picked up one of the statues and broke it, a key falling out of the middle and onto the floor. She bent over and picked it up, Eschina now breathing over her shoulder.

"What is this trickery?" Eschina asked, glaring at her.

"Why do you think it has never been stolen before? Because it is cleverly hidden. No one would figure this out on their own, though many have tried." She tried to back up, but Eschina wouldn't allow her. "Excuse me, but if you wish for the treasure, you'll have to allow me to open the door."

Eschina backed up, looking at the sheriff for approval, and he nodded.

"I need to open that door." Tara pointed to the farthest door.

They stepped back again, giving her room to do what she needed. After she opened the second door, she stepped inside, but Eschina pushed past her. "Let me see it first. You'll take something and hide it."

Tara shrugged her shoulders and allowed Eschina to do as she wished. This chamber was wider and held several pieces of furniture—tables, a pair of chairs, and other odds and ends. Statues were arranged on most of it, including the large chest of drawers against the far wall. Eschina rushed to the chest, opening the drawers as if the hoped-for gems would fall into her hands. A deep voice came from behind them.

"You'll not be able to get it." The two hooded monks stood in the doorway, their hands clasped in front of their full robes. Neither monk had belted his robe, Tara noticed, their sign for who was under the robes.

"The hell I won't!" Eschina rummaged through the contents of the drawers. She took out several small sacks, peering into each one before tossing it to the floor. "Where are the gemstones? The gold and silver? The mountain of coins?" She grabbed Tara's shoulders and shook her with fury, then produced a dagger of her own from her belt.

The sheriff held the torch flame out between

him and the monks, threatening to set their robes alight. "It won't take much to set you afire, brothers. Then we'll take it all. Stand back and leave us to the treasure."

One of the monks threw back his hood and opened his robe, revealing a large sword. He drew it and swung in a single smooth motion, cutting off the sheriff's hand at the wrist. The torch dropped to the floor and sputtered but didn't go out. The guard swung his weapon toward the monks. Free of the threat of impalement, Shaw launched himself toward Tara, knocking the blade from Eschina's hand and shouldering her to the ground. Eschina shrieked in pain and outrage.

The other monk threw his robe off and grabbed the guard, knocking his weapon away and throwing the stunned man to the ground. The first monk stepped toward the sheriff, but didn't seem to see the need of another blow. Though the man had clamped his remaining hand over the end of his arm, blood continue to spurt from the wound and onto the floor. He crumpled to the ground, and Tara knew he'd not survive—with no way to stop the bleeding, no cauterizing tool near at hand, his life would flow away with his blood.

Tara's brother Brin turned from the sheriff, shucked his monk's disguise, and tied the hands of the guard with a rope while Aedan, the second monk, took charge of Eschina, hauling her back to her feet and binding her hands.

Eschina, perhaps mindless with fury, kicked the sheriff as he took his last few breaths. "Nothing can stop us, you promised. You daft fool! And me even dafter for listening to you!"

"Hush!" Aedan commanded, giving Eschina a little shake. "'Tis no way to speak to the dead."

Shaw hugged Tara close, and she nestled into his chest. She hoped he'd never release her.

After a moment, they both turned to her father and brother. Tara said, "You cut it close, Papa. I was about to be forced to open the next door, and I didn't wish to do so."

The abbess appeared in the passageway. "I've brought our sheriff. Tara, dearest, are you well? Oh—" The sight of blood on the floor brought her up short, and she crossed herself. "May God be merciful. Lord Cameron, would you kindly arrange for the poor man's body to be removed?"

A flurry of activity took place around them, Aedan directing the local sheriff before leading Eschina the rest of the way out of the room. The lass cursed Shaw and Tara as she went. Brin found a rag nearby and stuffed it into her mouth.

"I've heard enough from you, lass. You will pay the price for your greed."

She attempted to kick Brin but he stepped deftly out of her way, and she nearly fell on her arse from the force of her motion.

The sheriff took charge of the guard and Eschina, leading them toward the entrance to the maze. "I could use an extra man."

Aedan nodded to Brin. "You go. We'll be up in a wee bit."

Ruari and his men arrived a moment later to remove the body, leaving Shaw, Tara, and her sire. Once they were alone, Aedan said, "I see you do indeed care verra much for my daughter, Matheson."

"You doubted me? Even though I was aware this entire event was staged, I still did not like a man with a torch threatening to set Tara's hair on fire."

Tara squeezed her arms around Shaw's trim waist. "Aye, Papa. I told you we were sincere. Why did you not believe me?"

Aedan shrugged his shoulders and said, "Watching a man leap to save you was a bit more convincing than your words, Tara. Much as I love you, I see he will protect you with his life. Every father hopes for such a man for his daughter."

Shaw kissed Tara's forehead. "Thank you, Lord Cameron. 'Tis true that I would give everything for Tara. But I meant what I said about setting all in my life to rights before asking for her hand. And now I find I must return to Matheson land to set things right. I'm glad we caught these two villains, but it did not solve my problem."

Aedan asked, "The sheriff did not admit to blackmailing you?"

"Nay," Shaw admitted. "He said he didn't know anything about it, and I believe him."

"He could have been lying," Aedan said. "If this part of his plan fell through, he could have returned to blackmailing you."

Shaw shook his head, then looked at Tara. "You heard them both deny culpability in that crime. Did you believe them?"

Tara looked up at him, and knew he'd see the

concern in her gaze. She didn't need to answer, but she nodded. "I don't think they are the blackmailers."

"That means that, unfortunately, I still have a blackmailer to catch."

Tara said, "And you still don't know what the lie is. Your sweet horse is still locked in lies. We have to uncover what that is about. The two must be connected."

Aedan shook his head. "I'm sorry, daughter, but there's no 'we' in that sentence. Shaw should return, and I hope he uncovers the bastards who are guilty, but you'll not be going along."

Riley emerged from the maze behind her father, breathing as if she had rushed to find them. "You found two of the killers. There are two more still out there, Tara."

All three turned to Riley. Shaw said, "But there were three here. Does that not mean we have only one left according to your dream?" Tara swung from relief to disappointment in the space of a breath. She'd hoped there was only one left to threaten her.

"Nay, sorry. The sheriff and Eschina were in my dream, but the guard they had with them was not. There are two other men trying to kill you, Tara."

Shaw glanced at her, and she could read the heartbreak in his eyes. She shared it, but as much as she wanted to be at his side, her father had spoken—she had to stay.

Shaw kissed her cheek and said, "You'll be safe here. We cannot risk your life."

She did not know if she could bear to see him ride away. Her father would agree to nothing before the issue of the blackmail was settled. But she would give Shaw Matheson her hand any time he asked for it.

For she loved him more than life itself.

CHAPTER EIGHTEEN

TWO DAYS AFTER Shaw left, Tara paced in front of the hearth in the great hall of Cameron Castle.

Her mother said, "You've been pacing since Shaw left. Much longer and you'll have to replace the rushes, Tara."

"I'll do what I must, Mama." She stopped to stare at the pulverized reeds beneath her feet, but then continued walking. "I wish Papa had allowed me to return with Shaw, and I don't understand why he had to leave so early in the morn yesterday. Papa could have sent three score guards with us. We did not even get the chance to look at the stars together."

The door to the great hall opened, and her father came in, Brin directly behind him. "Three score wouldn't have been enough to ease my mind, and I need plenty to guard here." He moved over to the sideboard and grabbed an ale before taking a seat. "And it was Shaw's idea to return so quickly. He is eager to resolve this issue."

"He talked to you for a while before he left. What was your conversation about?"

Her father smirked a wee bit, then said, "I suppose 'tis only fair for you to know. He asked for your hand in marriage. But only after he's ended the blackmail. I agreed with him that must happen first."

"Papa!" she said, throwing her hands in the air. "Why did you not tell me this before he left?"

"I was busy. I told you now. Why are you so upset, my lass? Did you think after Riley's dream that it would be good for you to hand yourself over to the villains?" Her father sat down and waited for her answer.

Riley came down the staircase and joined them at the hearth. "I can tell you why, Papa."

Brin said, "I'm quite sure I can also, but why doesn't Papa see it?"

Her father glanced from one child to the next, finally settling his gaze on her mother. "Do you know of what they speak, Jennie?"

Her mother smiled and said, "Aye, 'tis written all over her face, Aedan."

"What is written all over my face?" Whatever it was, she intended to hide it from now on.

Aedan raised his eyebrows in question. "Well? Tell me, wife."

Her mother glanced at her and smiled. "She's missing Shaw a great deal. They've been close companions for months. This is their first time apart."

Her father sighed. "I'm happy you've found someone, Tara, but could it not have been someone from Cameron land?"

Brin whispered, "Someone's in love!"

"Brin!" Tara shouted, horrified that the word had actually been spoken. But she was so pleased Shaw had taken the biggest step she could imagine—speaking to her father about marriage—that her insides were singing as if she were floating across the bay at Beauly Firth. "What else did he say, Papa?"

"He said that you had to marry him on Black Isle and that we couldn't come and that he wished to whisk you off to a kirk somewhere alone. And then he said he'd come back for you in six moons."

"Six moons!" She jumped out of her chair.

"Papa, do not tease Tara. She'll believe you, and you can see how much she loves him, can you not?" Riley chewed on her lips the way she did when she was totally exasperated with her father.

"Riley, tell me what he's thinking. I want the truth." Tara was ready to toss a hunk of bread at her father for teasing her.

"Sorry, Tara, but I cannot do that. He's teasing you. Shaw could not bear to be away from you for six moons. That I know without reading his thoughts," Riley said. "Do not be upset with us, sister. You and Shaw belong together, and you know how Papa likes to tease."

Riley's words settled in her belly like the most soothing words she'd ever heard. "Aye, we do belong together. Truer words I've never heard. Papa, I do miss him." She stopped pacing and fell into a chair. "I wish to return to Matheson land."

"Not until he settles what he needs to and you're sure to be safe there. He'll be back for ye. I told him to return once all was resolved, and we would talk."

Her mother shook her head in exasperation. "Apparently, your father has forgotten the time he chased me halfway across the Highlands."

"He did?" Tara hadn't heard this story.

"Aye. He followed me all the way to Grant land. Aedan, as a man who handfasted with his love before asking for my hand, you should consider that your daughter could do the same if you don't give her wishes fair consideration."

"Papa!"

"Father!" Tara and Brin both stood up, yelling different versions of their father's name in reaction to that news.

"Handfasted? You handfasted like Lily?" Tara's cousin Lily Ramsay loved to talk about her love of her life, Kyle Maule.

"Aye, we did." Her mother never lifted her head from her needlework.

Brin chuckled. "That changes everything, Papa."

"Jennie, I don't think you recall it well at all. I'm sure we did things properly."

Her mother laughed softly and said, "I don't think the tree near the loch where we rested would agree with you, husband."

Her father stood up, hands on hips. "Jennie, 'tis enough. No more sharing our secrets."

Brin shouted and pointed. "Papa, you're blushing. Look, Tara, his face shows Mama is telling it aright."

"Aedan," her mother said, setting her

needlework down. "They are all old enough to hear of our courtship. I loved you, you loved me, we pledged our souls to each other. My brother was too upset about Maddie to ever consider giving me away. Your speaking to him of it at that time surely would have caused him to have an apoplexy. We had good reason, and we married when we could. But do not think your daughters not capable of similar emotions. You need to consider Shaw's suit. Tara and Shaw clearly love each other, as you yourself noted after the incident in the abbey. I'm sorry circumstances are in the way, but they often are. Look at Brigid. She and Marcas in no way waited until all was peaceful."

"And Padraig," Brin added.

"You give good advice, as always, Jennie." He moved over to Tara, taking her hands in his and pulling her close. "Tara, you've chosen a fine man. He's honorable. I already know he'll protect you with his life, and he will be a good father to your bairns. But I'll not give him my approval until he's caught the bastard who continues to blackmail him. I suspect the person is not one but two, the same two who Riley saw threatening your life. Once that happens, your mother and I will happily bless your marriage. I just ask that you marry here at Lochluin Abbey. 'Tis tradition in our family."

"My thanks, Papa. I would love to marry here. I'll never forget Kyla's wedding. 'Twas one of the most beautiful ever."

"As was Connor and Sela's wedding."

Tara couldn't help but sigh about that one too. Sela's story had been heartbreaking, but she'd overcome the worst adversity, fighting for her daughter's life against the worst villains of all.

"I'll not disagree with you," her mother said, returning to her needlework. "The abbey makes a beautiful setting for a wedding. I hope to see you all wed there."

"I hope Shaw is able to settle things and returns for me soon."

"Brin." Riley's voice was breathless, and her eyes had glazed over.

Her brother moved behind her quickly in case she fell. Her head rolled back, her eyes closing, and then it was over. Riley lifted her head, the dazed look gone, and smiled, though it was tinged with worry.

"Do not worry, Tara. He's already on his way back for you, and he's moving quickly."

"Did he find the culprit?" her father asked.

Riley shook her head. "Nay, more trouble. They need healers."

Tara hurried to the healer's chamber, yelling over her shoulder to her mother. "I'll make sure we have the supplies. We can leave now, Mama."

Her father said, "Nay, you'll wait for Shaw to arrive. Otherwise, you'll not know what supplies you need. Or you could miss him, if he takes a different route."

Tara stopped and was ready to argue with him, but Riley held her hand up. "He'll be here soon. You needn't fuss."

Tara had to believe her sister. So far, everything she'd said had come true.

Everything but her own death.

CHAPTER NINETEEN

———————

SHAW RODE UP to the gates of Eddirdale Castle, pleased to see both his brothers there talking with the guards who were practicing in the rare sunshine. He'd taken a day before he left, just to spend more time with Tara and to speak with her sire. Then he left early the following morn, though he gave himself and his dear stallion more time for this return journey. Arriving home midday was perfect because he had plans. This was a glorious day, and the sun seemed a gift in honor of his good mood after talking with Aedan Cameron before his departure. He'd never been as hopeful about his future as he was that day.

"Shaw, I'm surprised to see you home so soon. Is all well? You know you were followed when you left, aye?" Marcas asked.

"Eschina and the sheriff of Cromarty rode out not a quarter hour behind you, but we trusted you and Aedan Cameron would soon notice them and keep them from any mischief." Ethan crossed his arms and watched his brother for confirmation.

"Aye, we saw them early on, so we had time

to plan. We had to draw them into the abbey through a back entrance to the cellar, making it easier to catch them at their plan if we were to accuse them of plotting theft. Aedan Cameron's clever trickery worked perfectly. Tara and I went ahead of the others into the abbey, making it appear we were alone, so they would feel bold enough to act. Everyone in the abbey agreed to play blind and pretend the villains weren't seen."

"But there were three of them and only two of you. How did that work?" Ethan asked.

"Aedan and Brin Cameron dressed up like monks and followed in their turn. All of us combined were easily able to overpower them."

"And where are they now?" Marcas rested his hand on the pommel of his sword as if he wished to land a blow himself, for all the trouble the sheriff and Eschina had caused them.

Shaw described how the ruse had ended, with Eschina and the guard jailed and the sheriff dead from his wound.

"Truly?" Ethan commented. "'Twas a nearly painless death then."

"And Eschina showed her true character at the end. She kicked the sheriff as he died. Such a warm heart I've not seen lately. Even Donald MacKinnie had feelings for some people."

"Why are you still mounted? Come inside and get some refreshment from your journey."

"Nay. I'm headed to speak with Dougal. I wish to let him know what happened and see if he has any suggestions."

"Eschina and the sheriff didn't admit to the

blackmail?"

"Nay, they both denied it and seemed sincerely puzzled by the accusation. Tara also believed them, and Riley said the guard with them was not one in her dream. There are still two more to catch."

Sammy came running down the pathway. "Shaw! You just received another demand for more coin. Your payment is increased because you did not make the previous one. Now he wants payment even more often."

Hell, but it had gone from twice a year to double that and now every moon? This was never-ending. Shaw shook his head. "This proves it wasn't them, then. They've been gone as long as I have, and Eschina is still in jail."

"And your primary suspect, the sheriff, is dead."

"I must speak with Dougal. Sammy, do you wish to travel with me?"

Sammy's face lit up. "Aye, I'll mount up, my lord."

"I'll go with you, too," Ethan said.

"Many thanks, Ethan. I'd appreciate your support."

An hour later, they approached MacKinnie Castle. They stopped at the gate, and Shaw called to the guard. "I'm here to speak with Dougal."

The guard didn't say anything at first, but then said, "I'll ask if he'll see you, Matheson."

They waited while the guard carried the message. "I'm certain he'll only see me. He's adamant about keeping this private."

Ethan said, "Understood. Sammy and I will see

what we can learn out here."

The guard returned a few moments later. "You only, Shaw. The others stay out."

Shaw dismounted and handed the reins to his brother. "This will not take long, I'm sure."

Shaw wouldn't allow it to take long. Dougal must have told someone about that day, of that he was certain.

Dougal waited for him at the side of the castle, and Shaw joined him.

"Back here," Dougal said, stepping into the shadow of a storage shed. "I do not wish to be overheard."

"I don't have much to say, Dougal. All I wish to know is who you told."

Dougal spun around to face him. "What are you talking about?"

"The Sheriff of Cromarty and Eschina followed the Camerons and me to Lochluin Abbey, intent on making off with the treasure that's stored there."

Dougal scoffed. "Fools."

"Aye. They both denied any knowledge of the blackmailing scheme."

"And you believed them? It had to be the sheriff."

"Nay, it doesn't. The man is dead, but I just received another demand for coin. And Eschina is locked up. It has to be someone else. I told no one the truth of that day. So the obvious question is, who did you tell? Someone else has known about it practically from the beginning. Who did you tell?"

Dougal's shoulders slumped and he shook his head. "Daft fool."

"Who?"

"Donald. I told Donald about a moon after it happened. He must have told someone."

Shaw couldn't help but scowl. Why had Dougal lied? Why not confront his brother about it while he was still alive so he could have helped discover the culprit? "I knew you weren't to be trusted. Mayhap you are part of this entire scheme."

"And blackmail myself? You are a fool, Matheson. Be gone. We have naught more to discuss." Dougal headed back into the keep, spitting off to the side, but then he stopped abruptly, spinning on his heel. "Are you still consorting with that Cameron lass? Why must all you Mathesons choose an outsider?"

"An outsider? What the hell does that mean?" Although now that he thought of it, Dougal had always spoken as if Lucretia would be no more than a dalliance for him. And she was from away, too. If he put his mind to it, he could probably come up with more examples.

"Why can you not find a wife who lives on Black Isle? You've all gone after the Grants and Ramsays, now the Camerons? What's wrong with the lasses who live here?"

Shaw scowled at him. "What difference does it make to you?"

"Naught. Begone. Forget I said anything. You Mathesons are not loyal to Black Isle. Now we all know the truth of it."

Shaw refused to allow Dougal's accusation to

bother him. He knew how Dougal thought, but he wasn't going to give in to his childishness. Was all this discussion about marrying lasses not from Black Isle meant to distract him from the original topic? For what purpose?

He turned around, knowing it was time to leave. He had much to think about on his journey back.

Someone was still out to get him, and that was far more important than Dougal's rudeness.

Or was it? Did Dougal have something to hide, just as he'd lied about telling Donald their secret?

He rejoined Ethan and Sammy, mounting his horse quickly and turning away from MacKinnie Castle.

"Did you learn anything?" Ethan asked.

"Dougal says he told his brother years ago. Now the question is who did Donald tell? Even that might not be an answer—once a tale is told, it spreads too fast to track."

They rode quietly for a few moments before Shaw spoke again. "Do you know what else Dougal asked me? Why all the Mathesons have to marry outsiders."

"Outsiders? Please be more specific," Ethan said, giving him his full attention.

"Lasses from off the isle. Apparently, he would rather see us marry MacHeths or Rosses or anyone but Grants, Ramsays, or Camerons. What think you on that?"

"He's afraid. 'Tis quite simple. Just seeing you fight against one of his guards probably upset him. You've become a powerful swordsman from your training with Connor Grant. And we've made powerful alliances. It means the MacKinnies have less clout than in past generations. Shallow men are afraid of any unknowns."

"You think so? Many thanks, Ethan." He'd never thought of himself as powerful, but his brother was right. "You think 'tis something simple like that? Jealousy?"

"Possibly. Or it could be worse."

"What do you mean?"

"He could be involved in your blackmailing. Who else could it be? If Donald told someone, the story would certainly have gotten out, as you said. But it hasn't, or we'd have heard. We'll ask Marcas. I'd like to think on it a wee bit."

They were about halfway home when two horses came flying toward them. It was Torcall and another man.

"What is it?" Ethan asked.

Torcall said, "Marcas needs you back home. Brigid has taken ill, and Jennet may have the same illness."

That sparked them all to push their horses into a gallop. They made it to the gates before they noticed the chaos outside, clan members gathering outside the gate, mostly those from the village behind the castle.

"What has happened?" Ethan asked. "Where is Jennet?"

"Inside," Alvery, one of the guards, said. "Marcas wishes to speak with both of you. We're managing things out here."

Shaw jumped off his horse. "What's the problem with everyone? Why are they out here?"

"They think 'tis another curse and want to go live elsewhere until the curse is gone. Any suggestions?"

Ethan said, "The cottages in the forest from the previous curse are still standing. But I don't see the need to run so far away."

They hurried through the gates and found Marcas on the steps of the keep, the courtyard nearly empty.

"What's causing it?" Ethan asked.

"We don't know, but Jennet, Brigid, Kara, and Edda are all vomiting. Nonie is helping, and I just gave the order that all water and anything fed to us must be boiled. Jinny said she forgot and served water from the well last eve, didn't boil what she used first. She's sobbing her heart out."

"What can we do to help them?" Shaw asked. He knew what he was ready to do, but he wished to hear it from Marcas. In his mind, Tara would be returning soon. Would her sire allow it?

Ethan grasped Marcas's arm. "The fruit tarts. We didn't have them last eve. The women devoured them."

"Our plan?" Shaw asked again. "Because I know what I think."

Ethan and Marcas spoke at the same time. "Go get Tara, and ask her mother to come, too. We must end this fast or we'll be destroyed."

"I'll do my best to convince them. I'm not sure Aedan Cameron will agree," Shaw said. "I'll take Sammy with me. We'll get some miles behind us before we have to stop for the night. I'll get fresh clothes and a bite of food, then go."

"Nay," Marcas said, holding his arms out to prevent his entrance to the keep. "Get food at Beauly. And bring some back with you when you return." He reached into a pouch on his belt and pulled out several coins. He pressed them into Shaw's hand. "We must be careful. Go, and try to return as fast as you can. Perhaps three days."

"I'll go as quickly as possible."

Another poisoning? Who could be behind it this time?

CHAPTER TWENTY

———— ❧ ————

TARA HAD NEARLY everything prepared for their return to Black Isle. Riley was surely correct about Shaw's coming for them. She had two clean gowns packed, some leggings and a tunic, and many healing potions fresh from her mother's apothecary. Though her father was right that she needed to hear why they were needed to know what supplies to bring, she had packed many of the more useful medicines anyway. Jennet and Brigid would welcome a fresh supply of their favorite powders and potions. Her mother was glad to share.

She'd paced most of the night, barely able to sleep, though Riley hadn't stirred. Her dreams and visions drained her, so Tara had resisted the urge to wake her, even as the sky grew brighter, though she yearned to ask if she'd learned anything new.

Her mother came into the hall from the kitchens. "I've packed some dried meat and a fresh loaf of bread for your trip. I still have my doubts as to whether you should go, but I know how much it would pain you to refuse Shaw's request for aid, if that is indeed what brings him."

She wasn't going to argue with her mother. Time would reveal the truth of the situation, and only then would they know how urgent Shaw's need was. Riley descended the staircase and joined them at the hearth.

"You're dressed already?" Tara asked. It usually took her sister at least an hour after waking before she dressed for the day.

"Aye, Shaw will be here shortly." She moved over to the trestle table and grabbed an apple from the bowl.

"We're ready for him." Tara wrung her hands and went to look out the door for the tenth time that morn.

"Riley, does Tara need to return with him? Will that put her life at risk?" Her mother's expression was calm, the calm Tara had always depended on whenever chaos reigned. Disaster could rage around them, but it rarely flustered her mother and father. Her mother always seemed to know just what to do and help others through the most difficult of events, and her father, once her mother's ways calmed him, would follow her lead.

Together, her parents made a powerful couple. She only hoped that she and her future husband could follow their example in the ways they worked together, supported each other, listened to each other, and used their brilliant minds to solve problems together.

And their love was evident to everyone. She often caught her father staring at her mother, a look on his face of such adoration that she was loath to interrupt their moment. And her mother always gave her father a wide smile when she first saw him after even a few moments apart. Tara thought it was as if she were seeing him for the first time, every time.

Riley's reply to their mother shook Tara out of her reverie. "We'll all be returning with him, the three of us anyway. I'm not sure about Papa and Brin yet. But there is sickness on Matheson land, and Marcas is worried. He sent Shaw to bring you both back, for your healing abilities. I go for another reason."

"I hope 'tis not another curse," her mother said. "Another malicious act, I should say."

"Why do you wish to go, Riley?" Tara asked. She knew she and her mother could handle whatever illness they found.

"I must help Shaw release Zinna from her chains. I must see this through, and I think he's close to the answer to that puzzle. He'll be able to discern the lie and who is guilty of it."

"It was not Shaw who lied, surely."

"Nay, not Shaw. Someone else is guilty of the lies and must face justice for them."

Silence settled over the hall as they each worked through Riley's information in their own way. Tara was about to ask Riley more about the liar when the door burst open and Shaw strode in, Sammy behind him.

Sammy babbled about their return while Shaw greeted her mother with a bow and Tara with a smile. Then his expression went grim, and Tara knew he was worried.

"We're hopeful you will return and help us," Sammy said. "The curse is back. Someone must have poisoned our well again and we have to boil everything and the clan members are leaving because they're afraid and…"

Shaw finally clasped his shoulder and said, "Slow down, Sammy. Take a deep breath."

"Who is ill?" Tara asked, almost afraid to put the question to him.

Shaw's face had never been more serious. "Brigid, Jennet, Kara, and Edda for now. If they don't get worse, they're in no danger. But just in case, please consider returning. Both of our healers are sick. We need your help."

Her mother nodded and said, "Have a seat, and we'll give you each a bowl of porridge with sausage, cooked fresh today, everything boiled. We always boil so as not to have that problem. You must eat something before we head back. You too, Sammy."

Sammy's eyes lit up. "Any fruit tarts? I heard yours are the best ever."

"Aye, we have some wonderful pear tarts. We'll bring some out. Any that are left, we'll bring along."

"Many thanks to you," Sammy took a seat while Shaw crossed to Tara and kissed her lightly on the lips.

"You wish to return?" he asked, his gaze hopeful.

"Of course." Then she glanced over at her mother. "Mama?"

"I'll be coming along. My sister would never

forgive me for not tending my namesake. And Brigid and her bairns too."

"And Riley will come also," Tara said.

Shaw's expression shifted from hopeful to relieved. He turned to Tara's sister. "Riley, you need not come if you are concerned about getting sick yourself. You could follow in a sennight, if they have not returned by then."

"Nay, I will go with you."

"I'm glad to have you along."

"Good," she replied with a smile. "Because you and I will be returning to the faerie glen. Once we are sure everyone is recovering and we've found the source of the sickness, we need to free Zinna from her chains."

"You can go ahead while we work on solving our problems at the castle." Shaw looked uncomfortable, his gaze darting about instead of maintaining eye contact with anyone.

"Nay, Shaw. You are the only one who can do it. Zinna needs you."

The look on Shaw's face broke Tara's heart. She didn't know how to tell him to trust Riley, that anything she could do would make everything better.

She lifted up on her toes and kissed his cheek. "You need to free yourself from the chains that have held you prisoner for so long."

Riley nodded. "We will free both of you."

★★★

They arrived at Eddirdale Castle late in the day, and Tara didn't like the scene that greeted them. A crowd milled outside the gates, asking questions about those who were sick. She heard one woman ask, "How many more are ill? Please let us in to see for ourselves. I'll not have my bairns die."

Torcall gave them the same response over and over. "Everyone else is well, and those who fell ill are improving, so you need not go inside. Go into the forest for a sennight or find a deserted cottage. There are many empty these days. They cannot all be full. Or move in with family for a time. There's still plenty of food in the garden and in the orchards."

Most accepted the reply, leaving with their shoulders slumped over. Shaw handed Torcall the reins of a pack horse laden with sacks. "Here. I brought this back from Beauly. Oats, barley, and dried meat. Share it out as you deem best."

Torcall nodded his thanks. "May I have some dried meat from Beauly? I don't wish to get sick either."

"Eat as you wish. We have more coming, but this we can pass out now to ease the clan's hunger," Shaw said. "Do not worry."

Torcall opened the gate to allow them in, and Tara couldn't dismount fast enough. She said a quick prayer that Brigid, Jennet, and the others were healing, and hurried up the steps. Her mother and Riley followed at a more moderate pace, while Shaw and her father—who hadn't been about to let his women go anywhere without him, with everything that was going on—had taken charge of their horses.

Inside the keep, she searched the hall for any

sign of her cousins. She let out her breath as soon as she saw Brigid sitting near the hearth.

"You are better, Brigid?"

Once she moved closer, Brigid held her hands up to stop her. "Not too close. I'm better, but still sick. We can't be certain if it's from something we consumed or a contagion, so please be careful."

"Jennet? Kara? The others?"

"They are also improving but sleeping now."

Her mother took a seat at the trestle table, a distance away from Brigid. "Though it seems unlikely, it could have been poison again. Mayhap directly into your food, not the well. We'll make a list of everything you all ate the day before you were sickened."

"We're boiling the water and being sure all the food is well cooked. We suspect it may have been fruit tarts Jinny made with water she forgot to boil. While she warms the fruit, she rarely boils it, and the men didn't eat any of them. But just in case, we're keeping the uncooked food under lock and key—boiling doesn't stop poison from working. We've tried guessing the source, if it was food or drink, and so far, the fruit seems the most likely."

"None of the men have caught this sickness?"

Jennet came down the stairs much slower than her usual pace. "Oh, Auntie! We're so glad you and Tara have come. Perhaps you can help us puzzle it out. It's true that the men have stayed well, so we're guessing the fruit, though there is none left to test."

"Jennet, you know your mother doesn't like

your testing methods for poison," her mother scolded.

"So true, and neither does Ethan. He made me promise not to." She shrugged her shoulders and gave her aunt a sheepish look.

"And you all fell ill three days ago? About the same time?"

"Aye, all within a day from eating the tarts."

"That could be the cause, for certes," her mother said. "While we think on it, I'll freshen all your supplies in your healing chamber. I brought plenty." She got up from her seat at the table and carried the load of supplies they'd brought into the next room.

"Do either of you need anything?" Tara asked. "A tisane or perhaps a cup of mulled wine?"

Jennet shook her head. "Ethan has been wonderful. I feel much better today. Brigid? How are you?"

"Better, and Kara seems completely recovered. I left her with Nonie and Tiernay in their chamber because she was into everything. I can't chase after her yet. And Edda has improved, though she's still abed."

Tara breathed a sigh of relief to know her best friends were improving and would soon be well. Now she could think about the other puzzles they had to solve. She'd been so worried about the sickness as they'd traveled that she hadn't thought to ask Shaw if he'd learned anything during the brief time he'd been home. Not that she would have spoken about the blackmail in front of her parents anyway.

"I'm going to look for Shaw, but I promise to be back within the hour. Send for me if you need anything."

"Go, Tara. You need not tend us," Jennet stated. "I fear your journey had little purpose, if you came only for us."

"I would have come for any purpose or none," Tara said. "Being back with you is enough."

She put her mantle back on and headed outside. At the gate, Torcall waved toward the bay. "He's fishing. Calms his inner soul, he says."

She hurried to the water but slowed as she approached. He was pulling in a fish, and it appeared to be a large one. He cursed at the fish as if it would respond to him, but she contained her giggles, watching him battle and finally land his catch. The sun was warm, so he'd taken his shirt off, which pleased her greatly. She took advantage and watched the ripple of his muscles as they moved across his broad shoulders. His hair blew in the wind, curling up on the ends. When he had the fish in his hand, removing the hook from its mouth, she moved closer.

"Congratulations, 'tis a fine one for dinner."

He glanced up at her with a wide smile. "Aye, Jinny will cook it up nice for us. There can be no poison in this fish."

"What kind is it?" Up close, the draw of his bare skin was nearly too much for her. His shoulders and chest were nicely bronzed, the slight chestnut-colored fur of chest hair drawing her gaze.

"A nice cod. I had a trout earlier, but it was too

small to keep. I'll let it grow a bit and catch it again another day." He glanced at her and smiled. "And I also have a cow in the other barrel."

She had to admit she was having a hard time listening to him when his bare skin was this close, almost near enough that she could run her fingers through it and down the line in the middle to the…

"And I plan to catch a horse next."

Her gaze shot back up to him. "What?"

He leaned over and kissed her cheek. "I like that you are entranced by my chest, but lass, you could listen to me too." His laughter echoed across the water.

She tried a playful swing at him, but he eluded her with one movement. "Don't worry. I look forward to the day when you can touch me all you like."

"And if I removed my tunic now and allowed you to watch my breasts bounce while I fished? Would it affect you?"

His grin disappeared and his gaze dropped to her chest, so she played his game and turned to her side, leaning back just a touch. "Why, Shaw, you look like you swallowed a cow."

"If I didn't smell like a fish, I'd grab you right now." His gaze narrowed, and she knew he was testing her.

She marched over and stood in front of him. "And if I grab you?"

Neither said a word, their gazes locked on each other. He lifted one brow, so she stepped closer and nearly grabbed him, but instead she leaned over and licked his nipple.

"Lass, you are playing with something you don't understand. If you do that again, I'll lose the last bit of control I've managed to keep around you. And besides, your father is coming this way."

She squealed and stepped back, turning around, pleased to see he was yet a distance away. Waving gleefully, she called out, "Greetings, Papa!"

Her father wore an odd smile, but he stopped a distance away and asked, "Shaw, you have something fresh to share for supper?"

"Aye, my lord. A nice cod. I'll try for another."

"Then I'll leave you two alone. And Tara?"

"Aye, Papa?"

"Don't be looking for any trees nearby." He chuckled and walked away.

Tara gulped on air, nearly choking, and turned her surprise into a cough. She would not tell Shaw what she'd learned of her mother and father, so she searched for something, anything to say to him that might keep him from asking what her father had meant.

"I didn't know you enjoyed fishing, Shaw. I know you've gone out with others with the nets, but I've not seen you with your own rod."

"Any Highlander near water learns how to catch and clean fish. Out in the wilds or in a drought, it can mean survival. Less so here at home, but it helps me think through problems. Since I'm not fishing to feed the whole clan, the line is enough."

"And what problem are you solving? Mayhap I can help."

He tossed the cod into a barrel full of water. "I need a couple more, if the whole castle will dine on them this evening." He played with his rod, but then sat on a large boulder, patting the spot next to him. "Sit closer to me, my sweet beauty, and I'll tell you what I learned." He donned his tunic and winked at her. "Just to put an end to your temptation."

She sat next to him, and he leaned over to give her a kiss, one of his thorough kisses that she'd missed so much. He pulled back before she could wrap her arms around his neck. "I'm too wet and covered with fish to hold you closer. I was not teasing you earlier when I said I smelled like fish." He showed her his dirty palms, and she acknowledged to herself that yes, he did smell more like his catch than she preferred.

"Aye, I see. Go ahead. I'm anxious to hear your news."

He took a deep breath and blew it out slowly. "I went to visit Dougal as soon as I returned the first time, and I asked him to tell me who he'd told about our experience. He admitted to telling his brother, Donald, but we have no idea who he might have told in turn, and obviously no way for us to find out now, unless he returns as a ghost as well."

"Did Dougal have no guesses, even?"

"Nay, and he doesn't wish to talk about it. He thinks the sheriff was lying, that he is the blackmailer, and it will come to an end."

"Could he be right?"

"Nay." Shaw explained about the new demand

for coin. "I have a feeling that Dougal knows more than he is telling, that mayhap he is more involved than it seems."

"Truly? But didn't you say he was also being blackmailed?"

"So he says. But I have only his word on it. Unfortunately, I don't know where to turn next."

Tara knew. He might not agree, but it was past time to complete the mission she'd been charged with. "I do."

"What? Tell me, and I'll do it." His gaze searched hers, and the little squeeze she felt in her heart told her exactly what this man meant to her.

"I know it won't make you happy, but I say it because I love you with all my heart. We must return to Zinna. I believe she will guide us to the truth."

He leaned over and gave her the softest kiss ever. "I love you too, though you're right—I don't love hearing those words from your lips. But I fear you may be correct. I'll do whatever you suggest."

"'Tis time to confront your past, Shaw."

CHAPTER TWENTY-ONE

SHAW DREADED RETURNING to the faerie glen, but he also believed it to be a good idea. He, Tara, and Riley rode out early the following morn, while mist still swirled between the trees and dew dampened their mantles.

Even thinking about it made him wonder if he was turning daft. A talking horse? Nay, a horse turned into a unicorn with the ability to send its thoughts to Riley. How she did it, he'd never know.

Aedan Cameron had insisted that eight guards accompany them as well, and Shaw was happy to have them. They would keep three as guards and send five patrolling while they moved into the glen. The threat to Tara's life still hung over them.

Shaw glanced over at Tara. "I'd like to go to the second waterfall, if you don't mind." It was a little more private, and it was where he found Zinna when they were here before.

"It suits me fine. Riley, do you care?"

"Nay. I think it is a good choice, since she appeared to you there, Shaw. It may be that the upper falls is easier for her to reach, as well, since she was able to come there without my presence to draw her."

"Easier to reach?" Shaw asked.

"When creatures, people or animals, pass on but wish to contact someone they left behind, they are restricted in where they can appear."

"Why wouldn't it be where she died? The place where we were hunting is a long way from here." Shaw needed to understand Zinna's appearance— the how and why of it most especially.

"Aye, perhaps if you or I went there, she'd appear. But I'm guessing you haven't been back, and I've no reason to go there. Spirits can come to faerie-friendly areas, even if they didn't know the place in life. In this case, it would be the faerie glen. Is there another on Black Isle?"

"Not that I'm aware of." He'd never heard of another, and he honestly had never spent much time in this area. Everyone knew the stories about it being a haunted place. Apparently, the tales were true. "Are there other spirits here that need help?"

"I don't know. They usually don't come to me unless they think I know the one they are waiting for."

They arrived at the glen just as the sun burned the mist off the surface of the water. Shaw jumped down to help Tara dismount while Riley pulled her horse next to a boulder and got down on her own. He tethered all three horses, then went to instruct the guards.

A moment later, Shaw, Tara, and Riley, with three of the guards right behind them, followed the path through the trees to the first waterfall. They paused to take in the scene, the spray of water making rainbows in the sunlight. The rush of the water and rippling against the streambank was oddly pleasing. No unicorn appeared, no horse, so Riley motioned them forward. Shaw took Tara's hand and helped her climb the small incline. Riley scrambled up after them before he could return to offer his hand.

They made it to the second waterfall, but Zinna wasn't there. "She was waiting for us before." He glanced back at Riley. "Can you tell if she is here?"

"Wait. I'll find her."

The three moved close to the pool of water at the base of the waterfall. A bank of clouds moved across the sun, the quick shift in weather that was typical of a Highland morn. The air was crisp and refreshing, though the chill bore the warning of winter coming soon.

Riley tipped her head back and closed her eyes, the slight breeze blowing the few free strands of hair around her face. In a moment, she smiled then lifted her head.

"She's coming." She pointed to a spot next to the waterfall, and the area shimmered for a moment before Zinna stepped through it, her horn already visible.

The beautiful white unicorn wore the gold chains this time, wrapping over her back and under her belly, but she headed straight to Shaw, whinnying and tossing her mane before she settled her head on his shoulder so he could stroke her.

Riley stepped closer and said, "Zinna, we need your help to discover the truth. Eschina and the sheriff were both caught trying to steal from Tara's friends, yet you are still in chains. Neither were guilty of the lie, were they?"

Zinna raised her head and turned to Riley, snorting at her.

"She says the lie still stands. You must remember, Shaw. She knows her chains are from the day she died, but she doesn't know the complete truth of what happened. She is counting on you."

Tara took Shaw's hand and squeezed it. "Go ahead, Shaw. No one else will hear. Tell us everything you remember. Mayhap some part of the story will come back to you."

Zinna turned to him and pawed at the ground.

"Aye. I'll begin after we met the lasses. I brought Zinna for Lucretia because her own mount had pulled up lame the previous week. I had my stallion, and Dougal had his. Eschina was riding a MacHeth horse. We moved across the meadow, then into the forest at different spots. Dougal killed the first deer, I brought down the second, then Dougal shot another. We had a wager on who would drop the most deer.

"Eschina thought we would leave after we dropped three—she was hungry, but Dougal refused to stop, though we declared him the winner. Eschina said she was leaving and asked Lucretia to come with her, but Lucretia refused, saying she wished to stay. Eschina left. Then I saw several more animals grazing in a clearing ahead of us."

Zinna pawed the ground.

"Keep going, Shaw," Riley said, resting her hand on Zinna's back.

This was where the story became difficult, the memories pushed down and down over the years. "I wanted to go into the woods on the other side of the burn, but Dougal led us to a spot where we would have to jump over a rough spot. It was a difficult jump. A tree had fallen just at the edge of a gully, but Dougal and I both made it over easily. I had no reason to believe Zinna couldn't make that jump."

Zinna pawed the ground again. Shaw studied the horse, wishing he could hear her as clearly as Riley seemed to.

"Does she agree she thought she could make the jump?" Tara asked.

"Aye. She knew she could and would not have hesitated had Shaw been upon her back."

Shaw continued, "Lucretia was upset. She was less skilled at jumping, and it was a more difficult jump than she'd tried before. But I wanted to beat Dougal, and I had faith in Zinna. I shouldn't have pushed Lucretia so hard to attempt the jump."

Zinna stepped back and let out a loud blow, swinging her head back and forth.

"It was not your fault," Riley whispered. "Zinna says you are innocent. 'Tis the true reason she has come to you as a unicorn instead of a horse—unicorns can only come to the innocent. She needs you to believe that the accident was not your fault. Go on. You're getting there."

"I was on the other side of Kinleigh Burn trying to draw the barking wolfhounds away because I thought they were upsetting Lucretia. I talked to her from that distance and told her what to do, that Zinna would get her across, but she wouldn't try it. I was about to give up and looked around for the shortest way to get back to her without getting in their way, and I turned back just in time to see them approaching the log as if to try the jump, but I couldn't see clearly. By the time I got around the bushes blocking my view, I'd missed the jump. Zinna was on the ground and Lucretia was screaming."

"Go on."

"Dougal was closer, so he said he would help them and I should go for the sheriff. I did what he said, even though I know now I shouldn't have. I should have gone to Lucretia myself."

Zinna pawed the ground again.

"Does that mean she agrees with what I said?" he asked Riley.

"Aye. Zinna said you should have gone to her. But keep going."

"When I returned with the sheriff, and it didn't take me long, I found Dougal with Lucretia's head on his lap. She was mumbling something."

"Where was Zinna?"

"Zinna was already dead. I went to Lucretia first. She was saying 'Dougal, Dougal.' Asking for help? I don't know."

Zinna backed up and reared with a snort. Her meaning was clear enough, even to him. He was remembering wrong or had misunderstood.

He shook his head and fought against years of resistance to allow the memory to fully return. 'Twas possibly the hardest battle of his life.

Tara moved closer and rubbed his arm. "Close your eyes, Shaw. Put yourself back there. What kind of weather was it? What did you see around the immediate area?"

He did as Tara suggested and closed his eyes, going back to that moment. He remembered how cold the ground was when he fell to his knees, how red blood had stained Lucretia's gown. Three bright lines of blood on Dougal's face from the scratches he still bore the scars from. He'd hardly noticed Zinna's injuries because he was so focused on Lucretia, her whimpering ripping his heart out. "Dougal, Dougal…"

Tara's voice came out in a calming lull. "Most people who I've seen die from a fall from a horse lose their life because the horse fell on them or they snapped their neck and died instantly. Or mayhap they have a large laceration and they bleed too much. Zinna was not on her, was she? And she was talking to you. So it wasn't her neck. What do you think killed her?" Tara asked.

"Her neck was fine. She could talk to me, but she was gasping for air. And she was bleeding."

Her hand tightened on his arm. "Tell me, Shaw. What did Lucretia say? Exactly. Repeat it slowly."

There was something…a niggling bit he'd maybe chosen to forget. An odd whistle came to him. No, that was not it. His eyes popped open, and he met Tara's eyes as he spoke the words. "Dougal did, Dougal did." At first he'd thought it was just the sound of the 'd' in Dougal that she repeated, stuttering in her pain, but he was wrong. It was a word on its own. "I could see blood in her mouth, and Dougal reached up and closed it. That doesn't…"

Zinna snorted again, as if agreeing with him. Dougal's action didn't make sense.

"Dougal did what?" Shaw glanced from one to the next. "I cannot think on it."

Tara whispered, "I think you must. Forget that he is a friend. Why would he close her mouth? 'Dougal did' means something. She was speaking *to you*. And he closed her mouth so she wouldn't finish her words. Think, Shaw."

His eyes widened as an awful thought popped into his head. Could it be true? A sick feeling swirled deep in his gut at the thought, but he had to say it. "Dougal did…Dougal did it? Dougal killed her? Is that what she meant, Zinna? Riley?"

Zinna reared up again, and one of the golden chains popped off her.

"'Tis the truth. Zinna saw more. More, Shaw. There's more," Riley said, her gaze watching the horse. "She still has another chain."

"How? How will I ever know the truth?"

"Zinna will tell you. Keep going."

The horse was calm again, but a chain still looped about her neck and legs. More lies remained to be uncovered.

"Where was she bleeding?" Tara asked.

"Her belly. She was drenched in blood."

"Could he have stabbed her and pulled out the knife?"

Shaw watched the horse as he spoke. "Dougal stabbed Lucretia?"

Zinna blew in a sound he recognized as frustration, and he almost smiled at the familiarity of it. She sounded just like she had in life, but the chain remained.

"Dougal killed her. But how and why?"

Riley stepped closer to him and set her hand on his arm. "Zinna can't tell you that. She has no way of knowing a human's reasons for something, and she can only answer to what she saw. She said that Lucretia was trying to rise when Dougal reached her, and a moment later, she was bleeding on the ground. But Zinna did not see exactly what happened. There is still a chain left. What are you missing? There's more that you need to sort out."

Shaw fought the need to chase Dougal down and put a knife in his belly. What had Lucretia gone through? Dougal had stabbed her in the belly, and Zinna had watched, then witnessed his lies. He spun around in a circle and let out a deep guttural cry of frustration, sending a flock of birds out of the trees. He turned to look at Zinna, tears misting his gaze because he knew what was next. Was it possible that Dougal had a hand in both of their deaths? Besides putting her down because of her broken legs?

"How? How did Dougal kill you, Zinna? I saw your broken legs so you would have had to be put down. That must have happened when you fell. But there was something else? Something you need to tell me to remove the other chain?"

He reached over to pat her withers, sensing she had so much to tell him but he had no idea what. The whistling sound came to him again. Dougal whistling. But he couldn't quite put the pieces together.

She nuzzled his hand.

"Dougal said he had to kill you. Your legs were broken from the fall. I would have had to put you down too. He did me a favor because I couldn't have done it."

"Nay, that's not right, Shaw," Riley said. "Not quite."

"What else could it be? I saw her broken legs." He had no idea what could have possibly happened. But then he remembered something. The pack of dogs. The whistle.

"What?" Tara asked. "Say it. She'll tell you if you're right or wrong."

He stepped back so he could look in her eyes. "Did Dougal call the dogs over when you were about to land? Or call them when you were in midair? The lot of them running in front of you?" His hand went to his forehead, so many thoughts now racing through his mind that he didn't know which one to focus on. The wolfhounds had been barking loudly just before the fall. Had they startled Zinna? "Did the dogs distract you?" He stood back, watching Zinna as her head tipped, then hung down.

"There's more. Zinna said he called Lucretia a word after she fell. Something she didn't understand. Something insulting." Riley moved closer to Zinna, wrapped her arms around her and rested her face on Zinna's.

Riley said, "He called Lucretia an outsider. She doesn't know what that means, but the way he said it was cruel."

He did. He knew exactly what that meant. Lucretia was the outsider. The first outsider. She came from off Black Isle. He wanted to grab Dougal and beat his face to a pulp, and then do it again.

"Tell me if this is how it went, Zinna. Lucretia decided to try the jump and started cantering toward the log. You knew how to do it, but right after you made the leap, Dougal whistled for the dogs, and they came running, one of them beneath you, mayhap, and you tried to change directions, but it was too late. You couldn't, falling instead, breaking your legs."

"Aye, go on," Riley whispered.

"Lucretia fell and hurt herself, but she was trying to get up right after Dougal sent me after the sheriff. After I was gone, he came over and plunged the knife in her belly, calling her an outsider."

Riley whispered, "He said, 'We don't want outsiders on Black Isle. We marry our own.'"

Shaw closed his eyes and tipped his head back, ready to bellow again. What would Marcas think of the situation? Or Ethan?

Riley continued, "Aye. Then he pulled the knife out and used it to kill Zinna. Lucretia scratched the side of his face when he stabbed her, but he slapped her and she fell. The rest was arranged for your return."

Tara whispered, "Outsider? What did he mean?"

"She was not from Black Isle. He asked me the other day why all the Mathesons were interested in outsiders. He doesn't like it. Thinks we should have all married someone from Black Isle."

Tara gasped. "Oh!"

Zinna stepped back, trotted in a small circle, then bucked, the final chain dropping off and dissolving to mist before it hit the ground.

"God have mercy." Shaw looked at Tara, then Riley. "I thought he was my best friend."

He hurried over to Zinna and hugged her, pressing his face into her mane, and the tears came. All these years, and the bastard had fooled him.

"Dougal's the one blackmailing me. He must be. He has a heart full of lies. 'Tis true. I know it now. My apologies to you, dear friend."

Zinna whinnied.

Tara said, "Riley and I will go back to the other waterfall. Come when you're ready."

The only other time Shaw had wept had been when his parents died during the curse. Now, alone with his lost horse, the tears flowed near as fast. The bastard had killed a beautiful young woman, her whole life before her, and a horse of unmatched grace. He wasn't surprised Dougal had lied about it, but then to turn it to his *advantage* and manipulate Shaw into handing over most of his coin made everything that much worse. The years he'd spent blaming himself were gone forever.

And what were the implications of his hatred of

outsiders? Had the sheriff been a partner of his? He thought of Donald losing Gisela to Padraig, of Fearchar MacKinnie staying in that small castle. Did they all believe marrying someone from off Black Isle was wrong? Had Donald believed it? Their sire?

"I have to go, Zinna. You know I must seek satisfaction for this." He patted her neck and looked at her, rubbing her ears and breaking out in a smile. "You're free. The chains are gone. Go to your rest. I'll see you again someday."

Zinna nuzzled his hand and then stepped away. She trotted to the side of the waterfall until the forest shimmered. She looked back at him and whinnied. Then she stepped into the shimmering trees.

When he could see her no more, he turned to the path.

He was going to kill Dougal MacKinnie.

CHAPTER TWENTY-TWO

SHAW MADE HIS way to the lower waterfall, then hurried to Tara, wrapping his arms around her and hugging her tight. He gave her a quick kiss and said, "My thanks to you and to your sister. Riley, this would have been impossible without you. I do not think verra many would believe our tale if we told them, but I feel like my own chains have come off too."

"I'm so glad you finally know the truth." Tara cupped his face, and he could see the tears in her eyes. He knew, just from knowing her, that her tears were from relief for him and sadness for their discovery, both.

"And you know I must go after Dougal. Now. I'll send all the guards with you, and when you get back, tell Ethan and Sammy to follow me to MacKinnie land."

Riley furrowed her brow. "Are you in control enough to go now? Do you not think you should wait?"

"Nay, I must go while it's fresh in my mind. I have to find out why he would do such a terrible thing. It makes me think he planned the entire outing. That he wished to make Zinna fall, that he wished Lucretia would die. That if she didn't, he would finish her." He didn't wish to mention what that meant for Tara, for Brigid, and for Jennet. They were all outsiders, and he had to see this to the end before something worse happened. "I seek justice."

Tara kissed his cheek and said, "Godspeed. I'll be waiting for you."

He helped the lasses onto their horses and watched them and the guards ride toward home. Then he took off in the opposite direction.

He felt as if he rode the entire distance to the end of Black Isle, though MacKinnie land was not so far. Whenever the way was clear, he pushed his horse into a gallop, and when he finally arrived, the animal was dark with sweat even though the day was cool.

The guard took one look at him and said, "He's not here."

"Dougal? Where the hell is he? I need to speak with him."

"He left hours ago with a circle of guards. Didn't say where they were going. Begone with you." The guard made a shooing motion as if Shaw were a stray dog.

Dougal could be on Matheson land or beyond, and Tara and Riley outside the safety of the castle.

Turning his horse, he kicked it into a gallop again. His blood curdled at the thought of Dougal hurting Tara. If he'd murdered Lucretia in cold blood, what would stop him from harming Tara or Riley?

No matter how he worked at the puzzle, he couldn't understand why Dougal would have killed Lucretia. Had his hatred for outsiders made him resort to murder? Why? There had to be something more there.

His thoughts jumped to many possibilities, but none made sense to him. He didn't think Dougal was naturally cruel, or Shaw would have seen it long ago. He still believed the murder to be a spur-of-the-moment attack. Though perhaps he was watching for an opportunity. Perhaps he saw the hunting trip as such, had paid off the guards for that reason. But why? Something else had to be driving him. His brother had turned daft over Gisela, but they'd all come to believe he had a growth inside his head that had made him cruel. Could Dougal have something similar happening?

Or had someone whispered thoughts of murder into Dougal's ear? Perhaps someone else had planted the idea. Perhaps it had all been someone else's idea. Including the blackmail.

The sound of galloping hooves brought his attention back to his surroundings. Ethan and Sammy topped the rise ahead of him and raced his way.

And he didn't like the look on either of their faces.

All three drew up together.

"What's wrong?" Shaw asked, the only words on his tongue.

"Tara's been taken by Dougal," Ethan said. "He had nearly a score of men. Our eight fought fiercely but couldn't stand against them. None were killed, but while they battled, Dougal stole Tara away and said we'd hear his demands shortly."

"Which way did they go?"

"I think they're headed off Black Isle. Away from MacKinnie land, at any rate," Ethan said.

"We have to catch them. Dougal killed Lucretia—all my memories have returned. Did Riley tell you?"

"Nay, she can't speak for weeping," Ethan said. "The whole clan is foul, then. We'd best find them as quick as we can."

"Did Riley know where he was taking Tara? Could she read his mind?"

"Nay, she said she couldn't tell," Ethan said. "Her father grilled her, but she had no answers."

"Where would he be taking her?" Shaw asked. "If not MacKinnie land—"

"I know where," Sammy said.

"Where?" Shaw and Ethan said together, turning to the lad.

"I'll bet he's going to the stable in Beauly. If he was the one blackmailing you, then he knows of the area beneath the stables. 'Twould be the perfect hiding place."

"Lead us on, Sammy. Ethan, go tell Marcas where we're going and get more men."

Dougal MacKinnie would die this day. He swore it.

Tara awakened to two yelling voices. She cracked her eyes open to see if she could guess where she was. It looked to be a tiny chamber in a cellar somewhere, a pallet, a pitcher of water, and a pot the only furnishings. The owners of the voices were nowhere to be seen—they must have been in the next room.

She lay still, careful not to make any noise that might alert them that she had woken. Eavesdropping might win her some answers to her tangle of questions.

Dougal and his men had come out of the forest so quickly that the Matheson guards had been taken by surprise. While the guards engaged, Dougal had come straight for her, scooped her off her horse and thrown her face down across his saddle. Flailing her legs hoping to knock him off the horse hadn't been her wisest move. He'd knocked her on her head with something, and that was where her memory stopped. And where her headache began.

She probed the tender spot on the side of her head and listened to the argument raging outside her prison.

"It's time you listen to me, Dougal! I'm your laird and father, and you'll do exactly as I tell you. Go to the Mathesons and tell them they are to give up the castle, all their holdings, and their title, or they'll never see Tara again. They've spent the last year ruining Black Isle, bringing all the new blood in. All these Ramsays and Grants—they're not part of this land or its lineage."

The speaker could only be Dougal's sire, Fearchar. The man was daft.

He went on. "The mercenaries I've hired are

positioned outside awaiting my instructions. If I need more, I'll find them. It amuses me that it's Shaw's coin that will pay them. The man has financed his own clan's downfall by paying us for years. I want them gone by sundown, and if they're not, we'll take the castle by force."

"Da, you have to give them more than a day to depart. You're talking about a couple of hours. That will never happen. And we'll never take them in that short of time. A battle like that could take days."

"Tell them they have until high sun on the morrow, then. Let them think themselves safe until then. Doesn't mean we have to wait that long. I've tried to be nice about this, but we missed our golden opportunity. We should have gone in when that fool poisoned their well and the clan was so weak. And this new attempt at poisoning failed miserably. Enough of all of it. I'm tired of waiting. We have the men we need and the reason they'll follow our every instruction. Tell them to get out or the lass dies and they'll face us in battle."

"No one knew the cause of the Matheson deaths during the curse. If we'd gone in at the beginning, we'd have drunk from the well and died, too. Waiting was the right thing to do."

Fearchar grumbled something she couldn't hear, but she heard the words "Ramsay witch" and "brother went mad." He raised his voice again. "This must stop! You'll do as I tell you, or I'll lock you up, laddie."

"Fine, Da. We'll do it your way. I'll send the

message. You're mad if you think they'll agree, but I'll do what you wish."

"I wish to control the entire isle. You'll have Eddirdale, and I'll have our land. With the Matheson holdings, we'll be able to hire more men, then we can move on to the MacHeths and the Rosses. The Miltons will join with us. The Mathesons can run and hide with their precious Grants and Ramsays if they don't like it. They won't fight back if it means I let you kill the lass in the next room."

"'Twould be a shame to kill her too soon. Mayhap I'll just tell them she's dead and keep her hidden away for a while, she's that bonnie."

CHAPTER TWENTY-THREE

S HAW HAD TO fight to contain his anger over
Tara's abduction. He had no idea what Dougal
might demand in exchange for her life, but Shaw
would put an end to it. All his guilt from Lucretia's
death had fled—he bore no more responsibility
than did Lucretia herself. All of it—the secrecy,
the blackmail, the lies—would end at the same
time as Dougal MacKinnie's life.

He'd kill Dougal MacKinnie with his bare
hands.

Shaw and Sammy were halfway between
Beauly and Eddirdale Castle when they saw a
group headed their way. Three men on horseback
approached and slowed, waving to them, so he
pulled up to see what they wanted. They wore
MacKinnie plaids.

"Message from Dougal," said the man in the
lead. "The Mathesons are to leave your keep
and give over your holdings or he will kill the
Cameron lass. All must be out by high sun on the
morrow."

That would never happen, but Shaw didn't
say so. "You need to take that message to the

chieftain of the Matheson clan. We have other issues to attend to."

The man grumbled something but then waved to the other two and moved past them toward Eddirdale Castle.

Shaw nodded to Sammy. "Lead on. The fact that they are coming from the direction of Beauly tells me we're on the right path."

"Aye, my lord."

Despite his anger and his worry for Tara, Shaw was looking forward to one small part of the coming confrontation. Seeing Dougal's face when he revealed that he knew the truth and that his plans would come to naught. He wanted their castle, but the Mathesons would never give it up, just as he would never give Tara up.

Ethan caught up to them a few minutes later. He'd raced to Eddirdale Castle and found a force of Cameron guards already checking weapons and mounting up. They'd explained Sammy's hunch, and Aedan Cameron had agreed that it seemed a good place to start their search and ordered his men to join Shaw's party. With their fresher horses, it hadn't taken long for them to catch up.

"We'll follow Sammy," Ethan said, and the Cameron guards fell in behind them.

Sammy gave a skeptical little laugh as they covered the miles to Beauly in a ground-eating canter. "I can't believe this entire situation has been over the takeover of Eddirdale Castle."

"Why can you not believe it? 'Tis what drives most men, control of more land, right down to our kings. They fight over who controls the Scots. Every man wishes to be the most powerful," Ethan said without looking to either Shaw or Sammy, with no more emotion than if he were discussing his favorite color of horse.

Shaw snorted. He didn't care so much about kings and their politics. Their actions had little effect on his clan. More urgent was the madness of the MacKinnie clan. "And so it is with Dougal MacKinnie. I'll beat his arse and put an end to this quickly."

"'Tis not to say I don't believe in you and your fury at the moment, my lord, but do you not think making a plan would be a good idea before we ride into Beauly?"

"Why? What are you thinking?" The lad was uncanny at times. He had a different viewpoint.

"He's gathered a good amount of coin from you over the years. I haven't noticed that he's spent it on himself—fine clothes or a new sword or any such thing. Why do you suppose he wanted it? And how could he have used it?"

Shaw had his ideas, but he wished to hear more from Sammy. "Your thoughts first, lad."

"He's done it to hire more men, just like they did when you rode in to rescue Gisela. Some of those men are still around, I know. Could be more have come. They did not hire so many mercenaries before that they'd not have enough coin to hire more now."

"Aye, 'tis true. And I'll not argue with you on that point. But they are not loyal like our clansmen are. If he has them, we can defeat them."

"But 'tis just a handful of us now. Mayhap we need extra help too. How many Cameron guards came with you?" he asked Ethan.

"Less than a dozen. You think wisely for one so young."

The lad had a good point, Shaw had to admit. No matter his prowess with a sword, it would be risky for their small force to take on a much larger one.

"I'll say it again. Mayhap instead of racing into Beauly, we should see what we can discover about MacKinnie's strength first."

Wise as Sammy was, Shaw's fear for Tara pushed him to speed above all else. He had to save her, first and foremost. But getting himself killed would do her no good. "Sammy, let's ride by the stables quietly and scout the surroundings. If there are guards, I'll guess you to be correct as to where Dougal is, and we'll need to gather our forces before taking action." He pointed in the opposite direction. "Ethan, take your men and scout the rest of the town. How many mercenaries do you see? How many MacKinnie plaids?"

Ethan nodded and headed off for their task, signaling the guard to follow him.

Shaw and Sammy rode casually into Beauly in the deepening dusk, as if they had no interest at all in all the extra armed men they noted posted in the streets. Sammy slowed when they approached the stables and whispered, "There's the stable. I think I can get into the cellar from the back."

"Keep moving, Sammy. I see men watching us. MacKinnie guards, if my hunch is correct."

Shaw did his best to count all the potential guards without looking like he was marking them. He counted about ten MacKinnie plaids, but more men were here, alert and purposeful, and it wasn't to find a wench at an inn and toss her skirts up in the hay. They stood watchfully at corners and in shadows. And he caught a flash of light against steel on one rooftop. Shaw motioned for Sammy to continue all the way through the town and to the end of the street so they could converse without being overheard. They stepped past the last building and turned a corner when something caught his eye.

A blue plaid in the distance, riding toward Beauly at the head of a column of men.

His spirits rose. A full score of men, at least. He motioned for Sammy to follow, and he stepped back to the main road to flag them down before they entered the town. Logan Ramsay rode at the front of the group, accompanied by his son Gavin, Gavin's wife Merewen, and nephew Gregor.

"My lord, you have perfect timing," Shaw said with a smile of welcome.

"Good eve, Shaw. Why are you here in Beauly instead of at Eddirdale?"

"If you'll come to where we can speak without risk, I'll explain." Shaw motioned the group into a clearing, away from listening ears. He suspected he'd been noticed by more than one MacKinnie mercenary. The Ramsay guards circled them, alert for unwelcome guests.

Logan, Gavin, and Gregor dismounted, and Gavin assisted Merewen before they joined

Sammy and Shaw in the clearing.

Shaw explained the situation. "Tara Cameron has been kidnapped. The MacKinnies are demanding we vacate Eddirdale Castle and Black Isle and hand over our holdings to the MacKinnies."

"Your castle for Tara?" Logan's gaze narrowed and he flexed his knuckle. "And my daughter and niece?"

"They are safe in the castle for now. Only Tara has been taken."

Logan scratched his jaw. "I was in Edinburgh when I heard someone from Black Isle was hiring mercenaries, so I thought it wise to return home. Then we received word from the Camerons that there was trouble again, but no details. I needed to see it with my own eyes. What is the issue this time?"

"This is between Dougal MacKinnie and me. I've been blackmailed over a tragic incident from some years back, and I've just discovered that Dougal is the guilty party. All this time, he's blamed me for a lass's death, when it was no accident but murder at his own hand. I want him badly, and with my fists, not my sword, if you can comprehend it."

"Och, I do, Matheson," Logan said with a grin. "The bruises and cuts on your fists will give you a sweet reminder of the pain you inflicted, but if you must fight more than one, use your sword. Take it from an auld man." He chuckled and patted Shaw's shoulder. "Who's the lad with you?"

Shaw introduced Sammy. "He believes there is a secret cellar beneath the town stables here, and it's likely that is where Tara is being held. He knows of a way he can sneak in to spy it out."

"We'd be pleased to assist you. I think we could create a suitable distraction to draw the guards' attention away from the stable and yourselves." Logan looked to his son and nephew. "Sound like good fun, lads?"

Gavin chuckled. "Aye, would be my pleasure. Find us a tree or two, and we'll start the entertainment. Catch a couple in their legs to slow them down."

Sammy's eyes widened. "You are the Ramsay archers? I've heard of you."

A second woman joined them—Logan's wife Gwyneth, Shaw saw when she got close enough. "Logan, let's move this along."

He burst into a wide smile and said, "Our lassie is fine and so is Jennet, but we must go rescue Tara. Are you not happy to join us?"

Shaw nodded to her. "My lady. Welcome to Black Isle."

She smiled and said, "Find me a perch, husband, and I'll get Tara free."

Shaw had to admire the woman known as the best archer in all of Scotland. She wore her leggings with pride, something that any other female would be aghast at. Instead, she fitted any female archer in the clan in her fine hand-sewn garb.

She whirled around and gazed up at the trees in the area. "Where are we to aim, Logan?" she continued. "I didn't wear these leggings for looks."

Logan laughed and nuzzled her from behind, giving her arse a swat and making Sammy's eyes widen. "You wear them for me, Gwynie, just because you look so fine in them when you're aiming at a target. I'll find you a tree as soon as I ask one more question."

"Fine, I'll wait over here."

"Any reinforcements coming?"

Shaw said, "Aye, my brother brought a dozen Cameron guards, who are checking the periphery now, and we'll have Matheson guards along soon, if they're not here already. I cannot wait for everyone. Let's move. I do not care to leave Tara in peril much longer. Not all the MacKinnie men are wearing the MacKinnie colors. Be alert."

Logan said, "Bring the battle on."

Shaw breathed a sigh of relief, mounted his horse and said to Sammy, "Let's go find Tara, lad. Lead the way."

CHAPTER TWENTY-FOUR

TARA LET THE two men outside her prison grumble and curse at each other, and even dozed a little to the background noise of their voices. As often happened in that half-sleeping, half-awake state, a thought popped bright as a star in the dark room.

She now knew who the four people trying to kill her were. Eschina, the crooked sheriff, and now these two—Fearchar and Dougal MacKinnie. They would not succeed. Shaw and her sire must be searching for her even now. They would find her long before the MacKinnies' deadline.

She sat up, driven by a sudden urge to fight back. She thought of her cousins and their own trials. Brigid and Gisela had both been kidnapped by men gone mad, and Jennet had nearly been drowned as a witch.

And the MacKinnies had been there all along, plotting against the Mathesons, against her *family*, both born and adopted.

The bastards.

Her cousins had fought back and won, and she'd do the same. She was not going to be killed without a fight. She gave a little humph—she was not going to be killed *at all*, if she had anything to do with it.

She stood up, removed her boot and started banging it on the door, waiting to see if it would bring anyone. Quicker than she expected, running footsteps sounded outside her prison, and then Dougal MacKinnie peered through the small window in the locked door. "Stop making such a commotion."

"I will as soon as you let me go."

"You're not getting out, so you can save yourself the effort and stop now, you troublesome wench."

"You expect me to sit here quietly and wait for you to kill me? I don't think so." She spit through the window and nearly hit Dougal in the face. That made her smile.

It did not make him smile. "You whore. I'll stop your mouth." He disappeared for a moment, the came back to the cell door with a rag in his fist. He put a key in the lock. Tara backed away from the door, ready to dodge him and run as soon as he came in.

"Dougal! Get over here now." His sire bellowed from the end of the passageway.

Dougal glared through the window. "You won't be going anywhere. I'll take care of you when I return." He flung the rag through the window out of sheer spite, she thought, and hurried away.

He'd left the key in the lock. If only she could reach it.

"What now?" Dougal shouted at his father. "I was busy."

"Ramsay plaids have been seen near the inn. They've come for her. Get out there and check the situation out. See how many Mathesons are here, if there are any Grants. The mercenaries won't recognize them."

"Any Matheson I see will be the first to die on the end of my sword."

"Stop your bluster and get outside. I'll wait here."

She heard footsteps on stairs—Dougal leaving the cellar, she assumed—and no one came down the hallway to her. After waiting a few breathless moments to make sure she'd be left alone, she put her boot back on and snaked her arm through the door's window to see if she could reach the key. She tried one arm, then the other. She tried flattening her garments, stretching her fingers, angling herself in the strangest way possible, but she could not reach the key.

Sudden fear threaded through her veins.

What if Shaw was the Matheson Dougal found with the end of his sword? What if the mercenaries *did* recognize all her friends and family and outnumbered them? What if she was left here to die and never found?

She screamed, the sound bouncing off the walls around her and echoing in her ears.

Shaw and Sammy led the way through Beauly, looking for anyone they knew. Halfway along the main street, they met Ethan and Aedan Cameron, the group of guards behind them, coming the other way.

Logan chuckled. "Och, but will this not be an entertaining evening? A pleasure to see you as always, Cameron. Any sign of where your daughter is being held? My archers will get in position as soon as we've located her."

Aedan shook his head. "I go wherever Shaw tells me to go. He knows this town better than I, so he'll be the lead on this."

"This from a chieftain who trusts verra few?" Logan asked. "Am I to surmise that what my daughter tells me is true? This man has been courting your eldest?"

Aedan gave Shaw a hard look before answering, "Aye, and I do trust him."

Ethan said, "A pleasure to have your assistance, Ramsay. We suspect she might be in the stables. Do you have any more information, Shaw, now that you've had a chance to look around?"

"I'm certain she's here somewhere, from the number of MacKinnie men around the town—we're not so close to MacKinnie land that they'd come here just to pass the time. We know there's a cellar under the stables that Dougal has made use of before, so it seems likely he's there. And where he is, Tara will be—he'll not want her out of his sight. Sammy said he thinks he can get inside to see if she is there. If some of you can distract the MacKinnies, it will be easier for Sammy to find his way in."

"Lead on. I'll find a place for the archers. You whistle when Sammy is ready to move."

Aedan held his hands up. "I think we need to

go about this differently."

"Go ahead," Logan said. "I admire your clever trickery. The ruse of your feigned death is still one of the best. Listen to him, Shaw."

"The MacKinnies and probably the mercenaries have noticed us by now, unless they are complete fools. I suggest we draw them to the opposite side of town and be obvious about it. Logan, if your archers are in trees and hard to see, their swordsmen won't know where to strike. They've no archers, so even if they spot any of you, you'll be out of their reach. Use your best banter to draw them farther and farther away."

Logan smiled, "I love this idea. Shaw? I think 'twill work better."

"I agree. Sammy and I will head toward the stable." Shaw turned to Aedan. "We'll stay hidden until you pull the guards away and we have a clear approach."

"Once you hear Logan's loud voice, then go," Aedan advised. "Godspeed and find my daughter."

Logan and Aedan gave instructions to their forces, then Logan led the archers away.

It was time. Shaw nodded to Sammy and they crept away, staying in shadows as far as they could, until they faced an open street and a guard between them and the back wall of the stables.

Logan's voice rang out to them. "Gwynie, you go into that tree, Gregor over there, and Gavin and Merewen can go to that side of the path."

The guard at the back of the stables shifted but didn't move. Shaw itched to go anyway, to simply kill the man, but he knew there could be more inside or around the corners. It would be suicide to try to take the building before the guards were gone.

Aedan's voice carried to them next. "Looks to me like you men are about to be shot up. Did the man who hired you warn you about the possibility of having an arrow hit you square in your belly?"

The guard they'd been watching moved to the end of the building, almost strolling toward the front, as if no more than curious about the ruckus from the street. It was difficult to see from their position, but Shaw could tell a few of MacKinnie's men were coming out of their shadows and hiding places to circle Aedan.

Logan shouted, "I think they're afraid of you, Cameron. See how they're keeping their distance?"

More of the mercenaries stepped into the street, all facing Aedan Cameron and away from the stable. Shaw turned to Sammy. "Logan definitely stirred them up with that comment." He grinned at Sammy and winked. "Where do you wish to go in?"

"About a horse length along the back wall, there's a large chute I found the other day, while you were away and I decided to do more scouting. I think I can shimmy into it. It goes directly to the cellar."

Another voice reached them from the street, presumably one of the mercenaries. "We were told sword fighting only. And I don't see any archers anyway."

Logan drawled, "Oh, well, if you weren't told, it wouldn't be fair of us to shoot at you." He called out louder, so all his archers could hear. "These men weren't told anything about archers. Throw your daggers instead, lads!"

Aedan teased, "Is that one not your wife I see? The one with the nasty reputation?"

"Aye, she shot a man in his bollocks once. Pinned him to a tree."

Shaw heard Aedan and Logan laugh, but then someone yelled, and Shaw heard running feet followed by the clash of swords. The sounds of battle erupted—steel on steel and the *whoosh* of Ramsay arrows hitting their targets, the yells of pain following.

"Sammy, lead on and hurry. I know not how much time we have."

They sprinted across the open space and flattened themselves against the stable wall. It was a large building, and the sounds of several horses shifting about and whickering to each other carried through the wall. Shaw assumed there would be stairs to the cellar inside, but they needed to move more stealthily, find a way in that Dougal might not be watching.

"I found it," Sammy said. "I can slip in right here."

The sounds of fighting moved closer—perhaps the MacKinnie men were retreating rather than following the Camerons and Ramsays—and Shaw knew they didn't have much time. "Go ahead, Sammy."

Sammy squeezed into the chute feet first, but

before he could drop, a scream tore through the night.

Tara's scream. It froze Shaw's blood.

"Go, Sammy. Now!"

Sammy dropped, a soft thud indicating that he'd landed...somewhere. A few long moments passed in silence from inside—no alarms, no more screams—and then a soft shuffle came up the narrow passageway. The lad couldn't slither back up the chute.

"Shaw!" Sammy called softly. "She's here, and she's unhurt. I can get her out, but we'll have to use the stairs. Dougal left the cellar a few minutes ago, but his sire is still here, so it will be tricky."

"Get to the staircase, and I'll come around and open the way from outside."

"Aye, my lord. We'll see you soon."

Shaw stood and ran, circling the building, and loosening his sword in its sheath as he went.

If he had to fight off ten MacKinnie's to get Tara into his arms again, he'd do it gladly.

CHAPTER TWENTY-FIVE

TARA WAS SO happy to see Sammy outside her door that she nearly cried out with joy, but she slapped a hand over her mouth before she made a sound. Fearchar had bellowed for her to shut up at her first scream, so she knew he was still close. A second cry would surely draw him to her cell.

If the old goat was still here. Perhaps the fighting outside had drawn everyone away.

She'd told Sammy about Dougal going out, and he'd nodded. "I'll be back in a quick moment, my lady. I must advise Shaw you are here." Then he'd disappeared again.

The rattling of the key in the lock was the first sign that he'd returned. The scraping of metal against metal seemed unnaturally loud, even with the sounds of fighting from outside. "Careful, Sammy. What's all that noise? Did you and Shaw bring guards?"

Sammy jostled and worked the key in the well-rusted lock. "Aye, my lady. Do not worry. There are Camerons and Mathesons and even Ramsay archers. Your sire is using his trickery again.

They're keeping the MacKinnies entertained on the far side of town for a while so we can get you out." Something in the lock gave, and the key turned. "I have it!"

One more twist, and the lock released, the door opening. They crept down the passageway toward the stairs. Tara's eyes searched for Fearchar, but he seemed to be gone. They climbed the staircase, pausing just as their eyes cleared the floor above. They were directly across from the stable door, which now stood open. It took a moment for her eyes to adjust to the dark of night from the lantern-lit cellar, but eventually, she could see figures in the street fighting, running, ducking. One man stopped in the middle of the street and let forth a great laugh, as if delighted by the battle. She thought she could just distinguish his Ramsay plaid.

"Ready, my lady?" Sammy asked.

"Wait. I see Dougal right across the street from us. We don't want to risk him catching us." Dougal appeared to be moving to a new hiding place, ducking as arrows flew over his head and not engaging any of the fighters.

"They were supposed to be on the opposite end of town. Why are they here?"

"Mayhap not all followed the lure, or Dougal called them back. Where is Shaw?"

"He's waiting for me to bring you out the door."

Shaw's voice caught her. "Dougal, you rotten bastard. Come here and fight me!"

He strode into view and caught up with Dougal

just as the other man turned and drew his sword.
"Fine, Matheson. I'll kill you right now. 'Twill be
easier to take your land."

Sammy let out a small yell as their swords
clashed.

"Hush, Sammy!" Tara whispered.

But her warning was too late. A shout reached
them from below, and she spun, almost losing her
footing on the stair. Fearchar MacKinnie barreled
up the staircase, his sword out in front.

"Run, Sammy!"

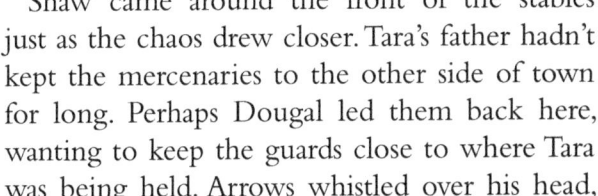

Shaw came around the front of the stables
just as the chaos drew closer. Tara's father hadn't
kept the mercenaries to the other side of town
for long. Perhaps Dougal led them back here,
wanting to keep the guards close to where Tara
was being held. Arrows whistled over his head,
finding their marks of the men on rooftops, while
the Cameron and Matheson forces fought on the
street.

A mercenary he didn't recognize blocked his
path, and Shaw's sword moved without his even
having to plan the blow. The fool cried out and
dropped to the ground, his sword falling uselessly.
Shaw didn't bother to kill him.

He had to fight his way around the next corner
of the stable, and one after another fell or fled
before him. He caught sight of Ethan fighting
well on one side of him and Tara's father fighting
like a demon on the other. When his next
opponent staggered away, Shaw looked quickly

around the corner of the building toward the stable door, where Sammy and Tara would be waiting for him to clear their way. No one at the door. But Dougal was directly across from it and moving that way.

He had to take care of Dougal first, then. Fine by him. He stepped out and drew the man's attention to himself, away from where Tara must be hiding.

"Dougal, you rotten bastard. Come here and fight me!" To his amazement, before Dougal turned around, he saw the scars on the side of his face from where Lucretia had scratched him. She'd marked him with his guilt even as she'd died. He'd always believed those scratches had come from his running through the brush to get to her after the fall. He knew better now.

Dougal reached for his sword, unsheathed it and faced him, a twisted grin on his face. "Fine, Matheson. I'll kill you right now. 'Twill be easier to take your land."

Shaw swung his sword in easy circles, trying to quell his anger with his former friend. He wanted answers before Dougal died. "All these years it was you. You put a knife in her belly, sent your hounds to throw my horse off. Why? Lucretia was innocent, no threat to you or yours. And to make me think I was at fault, so you could drain my funds? Were we not friends? You're a sick man."

Dougal stalked closer and laughed. "Friends? We were never true friends. It was always a big competition. And you don't know for sure I put a knife in her belly. She may have died on her own.

She landed on a broken branch, surely."

"Except I see the scars on where Lucretia scratched you, tried to stop you from killing her. I know what they're from. No thorn bush or branch would mark you so deep."

Dougal reached up to rub the scars. "How the hell could you have known that?" His eyes hardened, a determination settling on his face. And Shaw knew this would be a battle to the death.

Dougal swung his sword fast and hard, but Shaw blocked the blow automatically.

"How did you guess?" Dougal repeated. "I feared you saw me thrust my dagger in her belly, but you went daft as soon as you saw the blood." He grinned evilly, an expression Shaw had never seen before.

"It matters not how I know. You'll get justice for your crimes."

Dougal took two steps back and paused to answer. "Why? Because you and yours think you're better than the rest of us on Black Isle? You're ruining it, fouling the bloodlines by mixing our blood with the Ramsays and the Grants. It's past time for you to leave and let us keep our home pure. You tried with Lucretia, but you didn't get the message, did you? Why can't you and your brothers find a Milton or MacHeth lass? Leave the others off the isle."

Dougal attacked again, killing blows Shaw fended off and returned, forward and back, lunge and parry, neither one gaining the upper hand. Then Dougal caught Shaw's shoulder a glancing blow. He didn't even feel the cut.

He slowed for a moment to admire his work. "Blood. Such a beautiful color. I'll have your blood all over the ground, Matheson."

Dougal swung again, perhaps hoping Shaw would move more slowly now. But Shaw dodged.

"You aren't strong enough to kill me, Dougal. Too lazy."

"Spoiled man." Dougal spit at his feet. "Your father never treated you the way mine did me. You have scars on your back like I do? Like my brother did?" His litany of injuries continued as their swords clashed, again equally matched, neither giving way.

"Why do you want our land? Tend to your own and leave us be." His breath came short now, and it was harder to talk. His arms burned from the constant blows and the weight of the sword. No training really prepared a man to fight for his life, and Dougal was a stronger fighter than he had expected.

"We should have taken your land long ago."

Dougal slowed as he laughed, and Shaw took advantage of his blunder. He swung at his old friend with a ferocity that surprised him, and Dougal fell to his knees, but he scrambled back and got to his feet. Shaw moved in close with him again. With every blow, every word from Dougal's mouth, his fury grew. Murderer, blackmailer, cruel-hearted fool.

Dougal sneered. "Donald failed. I'll not. Your castle…will…be mine."

Dougal was weakening, his breathing grating

harshly, his words sounding forced.

His movements slowed, giving Shaw the chance he wanted, the chance to finally think through all that had taken place. "Your mistake was stealing the lass I love."

Dougal cackled and turned his head toward the stable. "My lass now, Shaw!"

Shaw plunged his sword straight into Dougal's belly. "You and your clan are done."

Dougal's eyes widened as he fell to his knees, his weapon thumping to the ground. Shaw wrenched his blade upward and out, and Dougal toppled into the dirt. Shaw wiped the sweat from his face and scanned the area for any other attackers, but the rest of the MacKinnie men were laying down their arms in surrender.

He turned toward the stable just in time to see the door bang open. Tara and Sammy burst out, running with makeshift weapons in their hands. Sammy carried a shovel while Tara held half of some broken tool. They'd been fighting someone, clearly.

Fearchar charged behind Tara, his sword over his head aimed straight at the woman he loved.

He was going to kill her.

Shaw squared up with Fearchar, his sword steady and strong before him. Tara's gaze landed on his, and he gave his head a sharp tilt to the left. He needed her out of the way. She grabbed Sammy's arm and pulled him to the side. Fearchar saw Shaw, but the old man couldn't dodge as quickly as Tara and Sammy, and his momentum carried him straight on.

Three arrows thunked into the man just as Shaw took his first running step forward. One arrow caught him in the neck, one in the shoulder, and one in the leg. He barely seemed to notice, only slowing because the third arrow hampered his gait.

Shaw raised his sword, bracing for impact. Then Aedan Cameron was there, throwing a log at Fearchar's feet, tripping him. Fearchar stumbled, and Aedan calmly stepped up, grabbed his shoulder, and plunged his sword deep into the man's belly.

"That is for my daughter," Aedan said, his normally hearty voice low and cold.

Tara launched herself at Shaw. He dropped his sword and opened his arms, holding her close and kissing her forehead. Tears streamed from her eyes.

"You are hale? He did not hurt you?" Shaw asked, moving her out of the center of the gathered clans, away from everyone's gaze.

"I'm fine. My thanks to you for saving me. I knew you'd come for me." She sniffled, then lifted her face to give him a kiss, but a man cleared his throat behind her. Whirling around, she took one look at her father's expression of chagrin and threw herself at her father in turn.

"Oh, Papa!"

Shaw smiled at their reunion and shook himself free of the fear that had ridden him, the burden of carrying old secrets and guilt for years. Aye, he was free now, absolved of guilt and unfettered by blackmail. Free to love a brave Cameron lass.

"Chief Cameron, you told me to return when I'd settled my affairs, and we'd speak of my love for your daughter. Now I've proven my honor, will you grant me Tara's hand in marriage?"

Tara turned back around and grinned. "Aye, he will. And I'll gladly accept your offer."

Aedan smiled and nodded. "Who am I to argue with my daughter and the man who risks all for her life?"

They were finally betrothed.

CHAPTER TWENTY-SIX

TARA RODE BACK to Eddirdale Castle tucked in front of Shaw in his saddle. She loved the feel of his arm holding her close and how he caressed her and kissed the top of her head, each small touch making her smile.

"'Tis over. Finally," he said. She could hear the relief in his voice.

"Fearchar was behind all of it, Shaw. Everything but the curse. The witchery trial, Donald and Gisela's betrothal, too, I think. Everything."

"Aye. And Lucretia's death, as well. Let's not think on it now. We both need to enjoy the night and the circle of family. We'll trade tales another time."

"That would please me indeed. I'm so happy to be back with you." She didn't even try to stop the sigh that escaped from her lips.

"We have many supporters with us as well."

"How bad is your shoulder injury? I thought I saw blood."

"That was barely a scratch. It will heal on its own, lass. Do not worry about it." He kissed her shoulder and waggled his brow at her, something she caught when she glanced back at him.

She listened to all the friendly cheers and camaraderie as they rode. Uncle Logan and Aunt Gwyneth led the way; she knew they were eager to see Brigid again, almost as eager as they were to see their two new grandbairns, Kara and Tiernay. Gavin, Merewen, Gregor, and the rest of the Ramsay group whistled and cheered behind Tara and Shaw, the two cousins' boasts about who was the better archer carrying forward with the wind.

When the bay came into view, the moon reflecting off the water, the group quieted, as if there was something sacred about the sight.

"'Tis beautiful land and sea here on Black Isle." Tara couldn't take her eyes from the sparkling firth.

"Does that mean you'll consider living here with me? We can visit your home whenever you wish, but I'd like to stay at Eddirdale Castle and help my brothers rebuild the clan, at least for a while."

"And a good job you'll do of it, too, especially now that the MacKinnies will no longer be a bother. I have grown to love this area as much as my cousins have, and I would be happy to make this my home. But I do have one request."

"Aye?"

"I'd like to marry at Lochluin Abbey." She glanced up at him over her shoulder and he waggled his brow, the look that always made her smile.

"I so look forward to a life with you, Tara

Cameron." Then his look changed to something more contemplative. "I will marry you anywhere you wish, and there's no better place than the abbey. Mayhap we'll finally have the chance to view the stars from the hill."

Once they arrived at Eddirdale Castle, she had to cover her ears, the cheers of celebration were so loud, echoing off the stone walls. But she couldn't help but laugh at her cousins' exuberant yells. Brigid and Jennet raced out of the castle and into the courtyard, the worry on their faces melting into delight and whoops of joy bursting out of them unbidden.

Shaw helped her down, and her cousins hugged her the moment her feet touched the ground.

Uncle Logan's voice reached them from the gate. "Brigid, your father's over here!"

Brigid laughed and stepped back from Tara. "We're so glad you are well, but we also have a gift for you."

Tara gave her cousin a quizzical look, and Jennet whispered in her ear, "A cottage set up for you and Shaw. We'll take you upstairs, then you can sneak out the back entrance while the revelry continues in the hall. You know they'll carry on for hours. Ethan will do the same for Shaw."

She glanced up at Shaw. He grinned like a lad, so she had to guess he'd overheard Jennet's words. She was more than happy to let her cousins' plan play out if it meant she and Shaw could be alone together for a time.

Brigid gave Tara's hand a final squeeze before hurrying off to hug her mother and father and usher them inside. She knew her cousin would find her at the right moment.

She turned toward the keep and found her mother right there beside her, tears streaking her cheeks. She dashed them away and embraced Tara in the tightest hug she'd ever felt. "You are well, Tara?"

"Aye, Mama. I was not harmed, though I am dirty and exhausted." She gave her mother a kiss and said, "Do not worry. I am fine. And Papa is here too."

As if summoned, her father strode up to them. He grasped her shoulders fiercely and pulled her close. After the crushing hug at the battle scene in Beauly, she was surprised he needed another. "We're all well, Jennie. Shaw and your sister's clan helped save the day."

Jennet allowed a final hug then drew Tara away, saying loud enough for everyone to hear, "Tara needs a bath and bed after her ordeal. We'll take care of her while you all go into the hall for refreshment."

Her mother smiled and whispered in Tara's ear before Jennet could take her too far. "I can venture a guess about what your dear cousins have planned. You have my full support, my dear."

Tara waved to Shaw as his brothers encircled him, then followed her overly bossy cousin up the stairs. Jennet gave instructions to everyone they passed, sending them running every which way. Brigid met them at the door and pulled her inside the hall, up the main staircase, along the passageway to the back of the castle, and then down again and out into the night. Jennet grabbed a torch outside the door to light their way.

Tara didn't say a word, too excited and exhausted for words, just followed them along a meandering path into Gallow Hill Woods. They came to a clearing, a small cottage in the middle of it. Jennet and Brigid spun around in unison, and Jennet said, "Ethan and I have agreed to share our cottage with you for this night."

Tara stared at the cottage then back at Jennet. "You and Ethan? You've spent the night here before? Relations?" She'd never guessed.

Jennet and Brigid both giggled, and they crossed the clearing to the charming hut. It was small but neatly kept, even the outside, though no one would ever guess someone was using it. Isolated from the other cottages, it had a thick circle of pine trees to hide it from prying eyes, the thatched roof blending in with the forest. There was also a well behind it.

"Ethan dug that well by himself. He didn't want to depend on any other well after the curse." Jennet unlocked the door, and they stepped inside. "Yours for the night. Here is the key."

Tara was in shock and instantly in love with the space before her. On the left side of the room sat a large bed covered with thick pillows and furs. The hearth was situated on the back wall, a chest of drawers next to it covered with a few neatly arranged goblets. A pot sat on the hearth, ready to be hung over the fire.

A table was set for two, a platter of fruit and

delicious-smelling meat pies just waiting to be eaten. A basket of furs sat on the other side of the hearth. To the right was a partition, and behind it sat a tub, filled with steaming water.

Jennet circled the space lighting candles. "Ethan built this place for us to have our own space. Sometimes he wearies of being amongst the whole of the clan. You are welcome to it for this night."

"How did you know to do this?"

"Ethan has his own magic. It was his idea, and Brigid and I arranged everything while he and your father rode to help Shaw. He couldn't get out of his mind how difficult Shaw's life has been because of Dougal. He'll get Shaw here, so climb into the tub and relax. You'll find some lavender soap and a clean night rail on the chest."

Brigid and Jennet came on either side of her, each leaning over to kiss her cheek in turn.

"Many thanks to you both."

"We'll lock the door behind us and give the key to Shaw. He'll be here soon enough. We ordered a bath filled in his room, so you have a bit of time to yourself."

The two moved over to the door, and Jennet stopped to spin around. "Oh, I heard someone say Shaw asked your father for your hand. Are you officially betrothed?"

"Aye. We talked of it on our journey back here. We're going to live here, but we're marrying at Lochluin Abbey."

Jennet grinned and glanced over at Brigid, who gave her a brief nod. "Congratulations. 'Tis wonderful. Do you mind if Ethan and I marry with you? We'd like to marry at Lochluin, too. We could have a double wedding."

"I can't imagine anything I'd like better," Tara said, and the three squealed with glee all at once and hugged again.

Tara sat by the fire and brushed her hair, both nervous and excited about what was to come. The fire's warmth on her bare skin kissed away the last of her weariness and stress from her ordeal. She knew exactly what was to happen. Her mother had made certain she knew how a man and a woman came together, and had explained that sometimes the first time could be awkward and sometimes a wee bit painful because of a lass's barrier.

She didn't mind a little pain or blood—she was a healer, after all—but she also clung to the rest of her mother's information. "Some believe it is only a man's right to enjoy the practice, but in truth, women have the ability to enjoy it more often. And 'tis the husband's job to help you seek your pleasure. The Lord made it pleasurable for both, so when you marry, be honest about what pleases you and persistent in asking for it."

She didn't understand it much when her mother explained it, but she and her cousins had a private session one night a few months ago when the men were gone. They'd gone into Brigid's chamber with two wine bottles, and the four of them—Brigid, Jennet, Gisela, and Tara—

had laughed until they cried.

Brigid had started the conversation by whispering, "I climaxed three times once, and Marcas looked like a proud peacock."

Gisela had squealed, and Jennet had laughed while Tara just watched them, wondering about it. Jennet had taken pity on her and explained, "You might feel pain and bleed the first time, and some women don't climax until after the first day, but when you do, you'll understand."

Brigid whispered, "Women tell us everything when they're carrying."

Tara could attest to that, but she couldn't help but wonder how this night would go. She got up from the stool by the hearth and moved over to the chest, donning the night rail Jennet had left for her.

It was then that she heard the soft knock at the door. "Lass? 'Tis me."

He was so quiet she wasn't sure it was him. "Shaw?" She opened the door and peeked out, relieved to see him standing there alone in his plaid and boots, no tunic, his hair still wet from his own bath. He'd shaved his beard too. Opening the door wide, she stepped back and said, "'Tis the loveliest cottage ever."

He took one step inside, closed the door, and scooped her into his arms. "I care naught about the cottage. I only care about you." His lips descended on hers, capturing her lips in an ardent assault. She loved it.

She molded herself against him, tasting the mint leaves he must have just had, loving the feel of his bulging upper arms in her hands. She teased him with her tongue, and he growled, angling his mouth differently, his own tongue delving deeper into her mouth. Why was kissing this man so wonderful? He ended the kiss and nibbled on her ear a wee bit, sending shivers rippling through her body. She clasped him as if she wished to never let go. He carried her across the room and set her down in a chair in front of the hearth.

"We have all night to enjoy each other, my sweet." He winked and said, "I suppose I should dry my hair by the fire so I don't give you a chill." He tugged his boots off, then moved over to the table and asked, "Would you like a goblet of wine?"

"Aye, if you please." She stared up at him, and he did the one thing that always sent her belly into flips. He waggled his eyebrows and grinned, the look telling her more than any words could say.

"I love you," she whispered.

"Tara, I've loved you longer than I wished to believe myself." He handed her a goblet and sat down, shaking his head. "For so long I believed I was going to be branded a murderer and never be allowed to marry you. And I wouldn't blame your father for sending me packing, so to say I'm relieved by all that has happened is an understatement. I keep going over all of it in my head and wondering if I imagined some of it."

She leaned over and cupped his cheek. "Do not worry. My father is verra happy with my choice for a husband. He'll not change his mind."

He set his goblet down and reached for her hand, brushing his thumb over her knuckles before he spoke. "I want you to know that I would be pleased to just hold you in my arms all night, fully clothed, if 'tis your wish. I do not wish to rush you. I am fully prepared to wait until we are married."

She leaned toward him and whispered, "But I'm not. You have pledged yourself to me, and I to you. God knows the truth in our hearts. Let us consider ourselves handfasted. My parents did the same, and now 'tis our turn. I've waited long enough."

He let out a bark of laughter and said, "Then your wish is my command. Whatever you wish, we'll do. Tell me when you are ready." He took another swallow of wine then moved closer to the fire, leaning over at the waist to dry his long locks.

"And I'm surprised you shaved. I liked your beard." She was curious what had prompted him to shave it off.

"Marcas told me to. Said a beard is too rough on a lass's tender skin. He said your parents would know by the redness of your skin if I didn't."

"Then I'm glad you did. I love the color of your hair. It looks truly red, lit by the flames." Would they have a red-haired lad or lassie? She loved the auburn shades in his hair, and hoped their children took after him.

"I'm ready once your hair is dried, but I do have one request." Forever shy about her generous curves, she just couldn't help herself.

"I'll honor it if I can. I promise."

"I'd like to put the tallows out before we get into bed. And I'd like to climb under the covers first."

She feared a laugh or a tease, but he said, "How about if I keep my head toward the hearth and you do what you need to do? I'm still fanning and drying, so you let me know when you are settled."

"I like that idea." She waited until he turned away from her, then she tossed her night rail across the back of a chair and climbed into bed, pulling the covers up to her neck. "I'm ready."

He turned around and she noticed his gaze stopped on her night rail and he arched a brow at her.

"Truly? I was not expecting that." He put out the two candles and then stood at the edge of the bed. He ran his hand across the folds of his plaid. "Your choice, lass. On or off."

His voice was husky as his gaze found hers again. The glow from the hearth made him look like a bronzed god, his broad shoulders flexing just a bit when he moved. She'd wished to see all of him for quite a time now, ever since the sword fight at the festival. Now was her chance, if she was bold enough to take it.

She licked her lips and whispered, "Off, if you please."

"Lick your lips like that again, and I make no promises on what will happen next." He dropped his plaid to the floor and stood for a moment, as if he knew she needed a moment just to look. She'd seen many naked bodies but none as handsome as Shaw. But she was used to old men and wounded warriors. Not this proud, hale man before her. And his eagerness was obvious.

His hands settled on his hips, and he whispered, "Lick your lips again, lass."

His eyes glittered in the light from the hearth, and she had the wicked thought that it might be fun to tease him. This time, though, she obeyed, slowly. His manhood grew—longer and straighter—in front of her.

She held the covers up and said, "Please join me."

"My pleasure." He nearly leaped onto the bed, barely managing to slip underneath the covers.

She sat up a bit and turned to him, but the covers slipped, revealing her breasts. She made a movement to cover them, but he stilled her hands. "Lass, nay. Please. You are beautiful, every part of you. Please do not cover your beauty to me."

He cupped her face and kissed her tenderly, pulling back enough to take her into his arms so they could settle. He leaned over her and kissed her, a searing kiss that told her how much he liked dueling with her. He nibbled on her lower lip a bit and she parted her lips, and his tongue mated with hers in a dance that sent sparks flying through her, a heat settling in her core that traveled to her female parts, starting a tingling and a need unlike any she'd experienced before.

This need was different. Stronger. The kind of need that made her grip his arms, squeeze his muscles. She spread her legs without a second thought.

His hand rose to her breast, cupping it gingerly, and she relished the warmth, and when his thumb brushed the peak of her nipple, she squeaked in surprise and pleasure. Her back arched on its own, pushing against him until she could feel his muscles against her belly, his hardness at the apex of her thighs.

"I have to taste you, lass. If you don't like it, just say so."

His mouth made a trail of kisses down her neck and to her breast, his tongue darting out to her nipple.

"More, Shaw."

He lifted his head enough to smile, then took her breast in his mouth and suckled her until she cried out. His harsh breathing matched her own, and she had a sudden understanding of what it meant to want someone, to need them so much that it couldn't be stopped. This pleasure, this physical form of love was new to her.

She liked it.

His hand moved down her belly to the vee between her legs, teasing her until she felt his finger nearly inside her. To her embarrassment, she spread her legs open for him and pushed against his hand. "Please, Shaw. Finish this. I wish for the pain to be over so we can move forward."

His finger eased in and out of her, then two fingers, then he kissed her again, ravaging her mouth, his breathing harsh and raspy, much like her own. She wanted him inside her, a feeling so strong she couldn't fight it. "Now, Shaw."

"You're sure you wish for this, Tara? If I make you mine, there's no going back. You're mine forever." He brushed her hair back from her forehead and kissed her there and on her cheek. "I will love you for all time, no matter what ye choose now."

"Aye. Now, please."

He settled himself between her legs and eased forward until he was at her entrance, moving a bit more until he was partially inside her. "Aye, lass?"

"Aye."

He went deeper, a long, steady sinking, and she buried her face in his shoulder. It didn't hurt, exactly. But his length, his invasion, felt oh-so-strange and wonderful. He stilled and kissed her cheek and her shoulder. "Ah, lass. This is paradise. I won't move until you tell me to."

He held his weight up on his elbows and she forced herself to breathe as her body adjusted to him, relaxed and flexed, like her mother had taught her long ago. And in a flash, she needed him moving again. Right now. She lifted her hips against him, and he smiled.

"You are so verra beautiful, Tara Cameron."

He began to move, and they found their rhythm, a pulsing need driving them together.

Tara wanted fast and hard, bucking beneath him, wanting more, needing all of him. She spread her legs even wider until he was buried deep. Her center screamed for fulfillment even though she didn't know how to achieve it. He reached down between them and barely touched her in just the right place, sending her tumbling over the edge, his name on her lips as she climaxed, gripping his arse, trying to hold him right where she wanted him. But he didn't even slow, and neither did her pleasure. With one last, hard thrust, he finished with a roar, seated deeper within her than she had imagined possible.

Tara had the sudden impulse to be embarrassed and shy, but instead she smiled. Shaw had made every moment wonderful.

"Tara Cameron, you belong to me forever, and I to you." He rolled onto his side and took her with him, nestling her against him.

Never had she been more satisfied.

CHAPTER TWENTY-SEVEN

SHAW WAITED A quarter hour after Tara left with Jennet, wanting to make certain they would not be seen alone together. He definitely owed his brother for his gift. The night had been more special than he could have ever imagined.

Tara Cameron was beautiful both inside and out, and marrying her would be more than he ever could have dreamed for himself, especially with all that had been hanging over him. His father had told him that when he found the right lass, he would know it.

How right he'd been.

He made his way to the stables first and found Sammy there. "Lad, where's Ethan?"

Sammy flung a forkful of old straw into the wheelbarrow and said, "He's looking for you. Both you and my lady Tara. MacHeth is on his way expecting a full accounting of all that happened. You're to join them in the solar."

"My thanks. I'll go inside." He dreaded this encounter. The man had lost Lucretia years ago and now his daughter to her own greed.

Timm dashed into the stable. "Shaw, MacHeth

is almost at our gates. What shall I do?"

"Escort him inside. He should be treated with all due respect."

He crossed the courtyard toward the keep, forcing his mind from thoughts of last night and focusing on what he would say to MacHeth. Ethan hailed him halfway across.

"You've heard that MacHeth is coming?"

"Aye, and Timm says he is here. You'll show him to the solar? Best if it's you and not me." Shaw slipped him the key to the cottage. "I owe you."

"Aye, I'm on my way to the gate now." Ethan paused for a moment and asked. "Were you as happy in the cottage as I am when Jennet and I are there?"

"Even happier, I'd wager," he whispered back, unable to control his wide grin. Ethan clapped his shoulder and went on his way.

As soon as Shaw stepped inside the keep, Marcas said, "Good. You're just in time. Brigid has gone upstairs to fetch Tara. I hear she knows a wee bit more of all that happened."

"Aye, so she tells me. We were waiting until this morn to share what we learned yesterday."

He didn't have to wait long before Ethan brought MacHeth and one of his sons through the door. Tara came down the stairs, Brigid behind her. Tara moved to his side while Brigid moved to Marcas's to greet their guests. Once they'd exchanged a few words, Brigid excused herself to arrange for refreshment to be brought to the solar.

"Let's go upstairs," Marcas said. "We have much to discuss."

Shaw kept his hand at the small of Tara's back, ushering her toward the stairs, but MacHeth's son stood stubbornly in place.

"Lasses do not belong in a laird's solar," he said.

Tara lifted her chin. "Know you what Fearchar MacKinnie planned all along? I overheard his entire conversation with Dougal when they held me captive."

"Peace." Marcas set his hand on Tara's shoulder and said, "Lasses are welcome in my solar, Solomh. I'll ask you not to question how I run my clan."

The elder MacHeth glared at his son, who gave a silent nod in apology. They climbed the stairs without further discussion, and at the solar door, Marcas motioned for Tara to go in ahead of him.

Shaw had no idea how this was going to play out, so he decided it would be best to let his brother direct the conversation. A serving lass came in with a platter of cheese and bread while another brought in goblets of wine.

Once everyone had taken their seats and partaken of the food, MacHeth spoke, not waiting for Marcas.

"If you don't mind, I have some things I must say first. I must apologize for my daughter's part in this entire situation. Eschina was wrong to try to steal from Lochluin Abbey." He paused to make the sign of the cross. "I had no idea she was in with the sheriff on this foolish scheme. She is being punished for her part in it, and I regret any trouble that came to you and your clan because of it. At present, she is locked in her chamber in our castle. If she were a man, she would be in prison, but 'tis no place for a lass. Trust me that her mother will make her life more miserable than any sheriff could possibly do." He made a motion to both Shaw and Marcas. "Word came early this morn about the fighting last night in Beauly and that both Dougal and Fearchar are dead. The MacKinnie clan members are asking me what happened—some have lost husbands and sons—and I know not what to tell them. I'm coming to you for the truth of the matter. I hear it was at the hands of the Mathesons, Camerons, and Ramsays. Please tell us what the truth is. You know how quickly tales are twisted."

Marcas said, "Thank you for the apology for your daughter. We hope she finds a better path forward. As for what took place last eve, it was a battle over Tara Cameron's life. Dougal and Fearchar took her captive and threatened her life in an attempt to force us off our land. Tara, the time has come for you to share your story, if you feel capable."

MacHeth looked surprised, but the four men in the solar gave her their complete attention.

Shaw took her hand in his and said, "Go ahead, lass. Tell us all you know."

Tara cleared her throat and began. "Dougal kidnapped me when we were returning from the faerie glen, Dougal and a dozen men on horseback. He imprisoned me in the cellar of the Beauly town stable. I don't think he knew I could hear their conversation, because he and his sire discussed their plans for me. They would tell Marcas that he was to abandon Eddirdale Castle within hours or they would kill me. My life for the castle. It was his belief that the Mathesons have fouled the blood on Black Isle by mixing with families from off the isle. Jennet and Brigid are Ramsays, Gisela married a Grant, and I am a Cameron. Dougal's sire wished to control all of Black Isle, but I think mostly, he wished to hurt the Mathesons."

"Control all the isle?" MacHeth's eyes went wide with shock. The man looked from Tara to Shaw and then Marcas. "And what about us? Was he bent on attacking our clan next?"

Tara nodded and looked to Shaw, the vulnerability apparent in her gaze. Her strength would carry her through. He nodded his encouragement. God's truth, he loved her for both her vulnerability and her strength.

Tara took a deep breath and continued, "Fearchar wished to take Eddirdale Castle when the curse started." She described the argument between Dougal and Fearchar, and Shaw was aghast at how close they'd come to losing everything. "I couldn't hear as well after that, but I believe Fearchar tried again to weaken the Mathesons by spreading the rumor about Jennet being a witch. Then Donald's madness foiled his plan to take Eddirdale by marrying into the clan."

As she spun the tale, MacHeth rose and paced, his hands on his hips. On his second circuit to the door and back, his hands fisted, and he spun to face the group. "The man was daft. I've thought it for years, but this…this is truly proof of his madness. And how did he plan to accomplish this without the coin or the men to handle the entire isle?"

He looked to Marcas and Shaw, but they both deferred to Tara.

"I'm sorry to have to tell you this, but Dougal killed Lucretia, and for the same reason. Because he and his sire deemed her blood from off the isle. Because Shaw was with them that day, he was able to blackmail Shaw for all these years, threatening to spread the lie that Shaw killed her. He had coin from that and used it to hire mercenaries."

Shaw just barely managed to hold his tongue. He was still in shock that Dougal had been the blackmailer and had killed Lucretia simply so that he would never marry her and out of sheer hatred.

MacHeth covered his face with both hands, then moved back and sank into his chair. "Lucretia was murdered? Didn't fall from her horse?"

Tara's expression crumpled into sympathy for the hurting man before her. "She did fall, but Dougal admitted to stabbing her while Shaw was riding for help. He forced the fall by sending his wolfhounds in front of the horse when it jumped. The horse, one of Shaw's finest, was also lost due to her injuries."

"And Dougal allowed my brother to believe he himself was at fault for your niece's fall from the horse. It has troubled him ever since. The man was truly ruthless," Marcas said.

Shaw could feel the tremor in Tara's hand and said, "If you'll excuse us, Marcas. I think Tara has had enough for this day. Tara, will you come away?"

She nodded and gripped Shaw's hand, so he led her to the door. As soon as they were outside, she collapsed against him and sobbed.

He held her. Would hold her the whole of her life.

CHAPTER TWENTY-EIGHT

TARA STOOD OUTSIDE Cameron Castle and stared across the landscape. Jennet stood hand in hand with her, Ethan and Shaw behind them. The day was glorious, a rare sunny day with just the right amount of crispness in the air.

Tears streamed down Tara's cheeks, and Jennet looked aghast. "You can't cry on your wedding day!"

"I cannot stop myself. Look at how beautiful the sea of plaids looks down the hill. I can't decide which colors are more glorious, the red Grants or the blues Ramsays. And look at my papa's new purple plaids just for the wedding. Are they not stunning?"

"What about the Drummond and Menzie plaids?"

Shaw and Ethan said in unison, "Or Matheson plaids?"

Aedan Cameron and Quade Ramsay, Jennet's father, joined them, dressed in their finest wedding attire. Her father asked, "What is this I hear about plaids? You know the Camerons are the best."

"I do love the new purple, Papa."

Uncle Quade snorted. "I think you know which are the most glorious. The blue. Always the blue." His green eyes sparkled with his usual humor. He leaned down to kiss Jennet's cheek and said, "But truly, you are the most glorious this day, daughter. You and your cousin. You both are more beautiful than any sea of plaids."

"My thanks, Uncle Quade." Tara glanced over her shoulder at Shaw. "I just adore my dress." Shaw's chest puffed up a wee bit. Tara was dressed in the purple dress she'd tried on in Inverness. She'd had no idea Shaw had returned to the shopkeeper and asked him to finish the alterations to fit her. It had a purple bodice with ribbons of gold crisscrossing over the front and trimming the sleeves. She wore matching ribbons of gold woven through her hair. Jennet wore pale blue, with a bodice that matched the Ramsay plaid, ribbons of silver in her hair.

At the sound of a door opening behind them, Tara looked back and gave a little cry of delight. "Mama, you are so beautiful. And so are you, Aunt Brenna."

The Grant sisters had grown more and more alike, though Aunt Brenna's hair carried more gray strands. Both were beautiful in the sun. Tara drank in her family—mother, father, aunt, and uncle—and felt herself supremely blessed. Uncle Quade, handsome as ever, looked much like her father. She tipped her head in curiosity. She'd never noticed before, but now that they stood side-by-side, it was more obvious. She glanced at her uncle then her father.

Jennet leaned over and whispered, "They look very alike, do they not? I've always noticed the resemblance between our mothers, but not our sires until today. Perhaps 'tis the light."

A rider all dressed in red plaid and mounted on a black stallion came toward them, two brown mares following. He came across the meadow and stopped in front of them.

"I'm here for my two lovely sisters. Are you ready, Brenna and Jennie?" Uncle Alex asked with a little bow from the saddle.

He would escort the mothers of the brides to the wedding.

Stable lads, including Sammy, looking proud to be part of the wedding, led the other mounts forward, ready to join the procession. Uncle Alex, with their mothers, rode in the lead position, followed by their fathers. Then she and Shaw, Jennet and Ethan would come at the rear.

Mothers and fathers departed. The stable lads with the remaining horses stepped up. As if all four had been stung by a bee at the same time, the horses all tossed their heads and danced back, tugging on their reins and refusing to stand to be mounted.

"I cannot hold him," Sammy said, being pulled away by the animal.

Shaw stepped up to assist him. "We don't need wild horses for a wedding." He grabbed for the reins, but the horse tossed its head and broke free, whinnying, and all four took off around the back of the castle.

"Shite, Ethan. What are we to do now? We

cannot walk to the abbey—they'd send a search party to find us. Look, everyone's gone into the abbey already."

"We'll fetch new mounts as quick as we can," Sammy said, ready to run off.

Tara smiled and put a hand on the lad's arm. "You don't need to. I suspect our mounts will be here soon." Now she understood what Riley had meant early that morning. *Zinna has a gift for you. Watch for it before you ride to your wedding.*

She pointed to a spot in the trees not far away, where she could see movement. She knew exactly what would emerge from the forest.

A moment later, four white horses trotted toward them.

Shaw reached for her hand and gripped it hard, and she patted his arm. "She wanted to do this as thanks for her freedom. 'Tis her blessing and gift for our day."

Shaw's gaze caught hers for a second, and his eyes shimmered with tears. The white mare in front came directly to him, nuzzling his hand before tipping her head to show the quarter moon—shaped mark under her right ear. No horn was visible between her eyes today.

Ethan said, "I wouldn't have believed it, but 'tis truly Zinna. How could that be?"

Riley came out of the castle behind them. "Don't question. Just give thanks and enjoy her presence. She'll be gone after the ceremony, but she says she's here to make you smile. Then she'll move on and let you focus on your new wife this day. Brin and I stayed back so I could tell you what Zinna was thinking."

Tara broke away and hugged her sister. Brin came out behind them and said, "Sorry we're late. Riley wanted to make sure you got Zinna's message. We'll ride ahead of you."

Ethan helped Jennet mount one of the white horses then swung into his own saddle, awaiting Shaw and Tara. Brin and Riley found their horses tethered and waiting peacefully and went ahead of them, Brin calling out over his shoulder, "You look beautiful, sister."

Tara reached for Shaw's hand again and asked, "Do you wish for another horse?"

He closed his eyes, then opened them, kissing her hard on the lips.

"Nay, my love. I'm honored by her gift. And I'll be the seer this time and tell you what Zinna is saying."

"And what is her message?"

"That you and I belong together."

EPILOGUE

Later that night…

TARA TUGGED ON Shaw's hand and pulled him toward the abbey. They were spending their first night as a married couple in a lovely cottage behind Cameron Castle, but she had other plans for this eve.

Tara had dressed in the pale green tunic and brown leggings her aunt Gwyneth had gifted her. She snugged her plaid around her shoulders for warmth and took off.

"I'll race you there!"

Shaw laughed and made chase, and Tara zigged and zagged, making her own pathway.

"You'll not get us lost, wife!" he yelled after her.

"I grew up running this land. I'll not get us lost."

When they arrived at the abbey wall, she held her finger to her lips to hush him, and they tiptoed down the side of the abbey and climbed the hill behind it. Shaw took her hand in his as they stopped on the flat top of the hill to look up. It was a clear night, and the partial moon cast enough light to see well enough.

Shaw pulled his plaid off and spread it on the ground, whispering, "Show me. Enlighten me, love of mine."

She laughed and lay back on the plaid, and one glance up made her laugh even more. "'Tis a most stunning night to stargaze."

Shaw settled next to her, grasping her hand as he took in the spread of stars across the sky. "I think they're especially bright tonight, in our honor. Truly Heaven's glory and a blessing."

"Look," she said, pointing overhead. "'Tis what my sire calls the giant ladle and the wee ladle. See the cup part there, and the handle on that end. He sent away for a book from Europe that explains the history of the study of the stars. Astrology they call it. People have been finding shapes in the stars for thousands of years. One looks like a bear, but I cannot see it. Brin actually picked out an archer over there."

They lay together pointing out the different shapes they saw, making up tales to go with them, and wondering at the vast number of possibilities the midnight sky held.

"I've not looked at the sky in this way at all. I think Ethan would enjoy it very much. We must find a hill to use on Matheson land."

"You've never thought of it when on the coastline? I would think it would be clear as ever there."

Shaw snorted. "Too busy looking in the water for fish, lassie mine."

"Which star do you like? Pick one and name

it."

"There," he said after a brief pause and perusal of the sky. "That is the brightest star, and I'm naming it Tara."

He rolled over and settled himself on top of her, resting his weight on his elbows and cupping her face. "You are my brightest star, Tara Cameron."

THE END

DEAR READER,
Thank you for reading the last entry in the Highland Healers series.

I know what you're going to ask me. What about Riley?

I rarely end a series. For instance, you thought Clan Grant was finished, and then I added the ninth book, the Christmas novella Yuletide Angels. I like to leave a series open, just in case. I can foresee a story about Riley in the future, but she's too young right now, so I think it will wait.

Next up is another collaboration with my writer friends, Emma Prince and Cecelia Mecca. This trilogy is not a time travel, but a delicious story about a typical Highland clan feud set in 13th century Scotland.

And after that? Who knows? Even I don't yet.

Happy reading!

Keira Montclair

https://keiramontclair.com

NOVELS BY KEIRA MONTCLAIR

HIGHLAND HEALERS
THE CURSE OF BLACK ISLE
THE WITCH OF BLACK ISLE
THE SCOURGE OF BLACK ISLE
THE GHOSTS OF BLACK ISLE

THE CLAN GRANT SERIES
#1- RESCUED BY A HIGHLANDER-
Alex and Maddie
#2- HEALING A HIGHLANDER'S HEART-
Brenna and Quade
#3- LOVE LETTERS FROM LARGS-
Brodie and Celestina
#4-JOURNEY TO THE HIGHLANDS-
Robbie and Caralyn
#5-HIGHLAND SPARKS-
Logan and Gwyneth
#6-MY DESPERATE HIGHLANDER-
Micheil and Diana
#7-THE BRIGHTEST STAR IN THE
HIGHLANDS-
Jennie and Aedan
#8- HIGHLAND HARMONY-
Avelina and Drew
#9-YULETIDE ANGELS

ABOUT THE AUTHOR

Keira Montclair is the pen name of an author who lives in South Carolina with her husband. She loves to write fast-paced, emotional romance, especially with children as secondary characters.

When she's not writing, she loves to spend time with her grandchildren. She's worked as a high school math teacher, a registered nurse, and an office manager. She loves ballet, mathematics, puzzles, learning anything new, and creating new characters for her readers to fall in love with.

She writes historical romantic suspense. Her best-selling series is a family saga that follows two medieval Scottish clans through four generations and now numbers over thirty books.

Contact her through her website:
www.keiramontclair.com.

www.ingramcontent.com/pod-product-compliance
Lightning Source LLC
Chambersburg PA
CBHW070855180626
46817CB00003B/781